T0049282

Blue Crystal

Copyright © 2019 by Mark Ridler.

Library of Congress Control Number: 2019903506
ISBN: Hardcover   978-1-9845-8918-7
                 Softcover   978-1-9845-8917-0
                 eBook   978-1-9845-8916-3

All rights reserved. No part of this book may be reproduced or transmitted in any form or by any means, electronic or mechanical, including photocopying, recording, or by any information storage and retrieval system, without permission in writing from the copyright owner.

This is a work of fiction. Names, characters, places and incidents either are the product of the author's imagination or are used fictitiously, and any resemblance to any actual persons, living or dead, events, or locales is entirely coincidental.

Any people depicted in stock imagery provided by Getty Images are models, and such images are being used for illustrative purposes only. Certain stock imagery © Getty Images.

Print information available on the last page.

Rev. date: 03/26/2019

To order additional copies of this book, contact:
Xlibris
800-056-3182
www.Xlibrispublishing.co.uk
Orders@Xlibrispublishing.co.uk
793697

CONTENTS

EXETER OPERATIONS

Exeter is a city of great antiquity and fame, renowned for its loyalty and zeal for monarchy amidst all revolution.

Not anymore.

The crowds were camped out on Grace Road South, opposite the new Energy Recovery Facility on Marsh Barton. And if their banners were anything to go by, they were definitely not on the side of Her Majesty's Government.

'END THE HUM'. 'THE HUM STOPS NOW'. 'SHAME ON THE GOVERNMENT'. 'NO MORE HEADACHES'.

The people managing the facility didn't know what to do. They struggled to drive to work in the morning and had to stand guard on the gates to stop the masses from pouring in. Their management assured the crowd that they were operating no more than an energy processing plant as per the design, and that the rest was a conspiracy theory. At one point, they even offered guided tours of the building, a dozen at a time, but because the people didn't really know what they were looking at, this did nothing to dispel the rumours.

It made the news in the local rag, the *Express and Echo*. Crowd members had been interviewed and reported a variety of symptoms from hearing a low-level humming noise, to headaches, to hearing sounds and seeing flashes of light. Some even reported hearing voices, but they were advised to seek psychiatric care.

The *Echo* had then conducted a poll across a sample of 5,000 city members. Initial results indicated roughly 10 per cent of the population had experienced something, but it was thought that numbers in the St Thomas area could be higher because of the close proximity to Marsh Barton. A second poll was under way by the time the story made it as far as the national press.

*   *   *

In London, David Cameron, the prime minister, held a meeting with his top-level security advisers. They assured him that what was going on in Exeter was nothing more than some local hysteria, and that it would all blow over soon. They even offered him the chance to turn up in person and take a tour of the Energy Recovery Facility himself. This he declined to do for the time being.

*   *   *

Behind the crowd, a man stood watching. He was dressed casually in jeans and a leather jacket, to be known as 'Leather Jacket Man' or LJM from here on. He didn't know what to make of the claims surrounding the waste plant. But he knew what he had experienced, and it was an increasing number of flashes and voices in his head. Not all the time but at unpredictable moments. On the last such occasion, his experience had coincided with the crowd's reaction to The Hum. That was three days ago, and it had been seemingly quiet since then.

*   *   *

Two security guards stood outside one of the industrial units on Marsh Barton. They were on Hennock Road North, a short distance from Grace Road South but far enough away to have peace and quiet. They chuckled amongst themselves that they were lucky not to get that kind of hassle. They had absolutely no idea what their industrial unit contained, just that they were employed by the local security firm, Secure Force UK, to watch over it. They had noticed that when employees turned up, they tended to stay for days at a time, living off on pizza deliveries and stuff from Sainsbury's, which was all a bit weird. And they tended to speak with a North American accent too.

*   *   *

In a top-secret location in mainland USA, a meeting was in progress. The project manager, Jack, was a long way from happy.

'I thought the whole point of moving the operation from the USA to the UK was so that we could get rid of The Hum rumours once and for all. I was told we had the technology to send the EM pulse below the audible threshold. Yet here we are in the exact same situation all over again with the crowd running riot. What the hell is going on over there?' he demanded.

'Boss, if you remember, we moved to mainland UK because that's where our data told us the *strongest receiver* is located. We've managed to track him or her to Exeter, after a series of successful operations in London and Honiton. However, the situation in Exeter is different. It's way more chaotic, and the local population are responding to our signals much more. We tried turning down the audible level some more, but that increased the synchronicity of the pulse and led to reports of simultaneous headaches. For some reason, they've put two and two together and deduced that the source of the headaches and The Hum is in Marsh Barton. And they've bought the cover story that it's the Energy Recovery Facility, which has absolutely no idea what's going on. The situation is manageable, we just need to keep our cool,' reassured Theo.

'And meanwhile the *strongest receiver* is still out there. We're talking about someone with weapons grade military potential here so it's absolutely imperative that we find them. Project Blue Crystal will be for nothing if we fail to track them down. What's the latest on our technology then? Remind me what we have in place,' asked Jack.

'Boss, we have an electromagnetic (EM) pulse generator in a secure industrial unit in Exeter. It's big enough to disrupt communications in the whole city. So far, we've only used it over a radius of two kilometres, which is enough to take out of the Cedars mental hospital. The hospital is on the other side of the river with few inhabitants in between because of the Riverside Valley Park. It does mean we incur collateral damage in the St Thomas area on the other side of Alphington Road, which is one of the main routes into the city; hence, the crowd. However, we couldn't find any units closer, with enough industry in the area to make a decent cover story,' responded Theo.

'We also have a much more localised quantum entanglement (QE) generator in a house opposite the Cedars. At top power, we estimate a radius of 800 metres, which is enough to cover the old mental hospital Wonford House and parts of the main Wonford Hospital, with collateral damage in the Burnthouse Lane area. Rather embarrassingly, that also includes the military base on Barrack Road,' added Laura.

'All operations in London and Honiton have been disbanded. We still have a QE generator in Honiton, but it's an older model, and we took the opportunity to upgrade for the Exeter op. Security is still watching over it but the cost-benefit of moving it is probably not worth the risk because we think some of the people affected are still scouting the area,' said Albert.

'Since moving the operations from the USA to the UK, we've had the benefit of HQ being separated at a much greater distance, which considerably reduces the collateral damage here. So we expect to have way fewer headaches and a much lower turnover of staff from here on,' added Nicky.

'What have we found out from the local hospital?' continued Jack

'Boss, as I'm sure you've already been briefed, we know that the strongest receivers are people with mental health issues. In particular, psychosis sufferers are well known to hear voices and see things that the rest of us don't. There is still some suspicion that much of what they experience is psychosomatic, but we've been able to prove definitely that some of what they receive includes signals sent by us. We're talking people with schizophrenia, bipolar disorder, and some with borderline personality disorder. The ones with schizophrenia, experience symptoms the whole time, so it's hard weeding out the signals. Whereas the others have episodes where they experience symptoms and then get better again. They seem to be the most promising for discerning between signals, but it's early days,' summarised Nicky.

'We've redone the strongest receiver analysis and it's come back loud and clear that Exeter is the right place. So it's looking like we won't need to move operations again. However, to date, we have absolutely no idea who we're looking for. Male or female? Age unknown. It could even be a group of people who are collectively fielding the most signals. We'll need a much longer pulse signal if you want to localise things more. Right now, we know they're within the city boundary, but that's about it,' established Albert.

'In contrast, the strongest senders are basically celebrities. Because people have already heard about them, there is a ready-made connection waiting to be used. The only trouble is that the celebs have absolutely no discernment, and so send their signal to everyone in the target radius. To date, we've made no progress in narrowing that down. We've used B-list people to try and keep the visibility down. If you want to go to A-list, it's going to raise a lot more eyebrows. And nobody is going to thank us if we take out Madonna with a massive headache. Perhaps a more promising route going forward would be to select celebrities with mental health disorders. Then we could do a combined Send and Receive Analysis,' suggested Nicky.

'I can see this is a huge security nightmare. Well done for keeping it under wraps as of to date. I'm going to have to go upstairs before I authorise any of these moves. In the meantime, I assume we can carry on local ops at the Cedars if we stick with the B-list for now, at the risk of needing another EM pulse to clear up the mess. Which will mean more crowd. On the subject of which, are there any ideas on how to plant some alternative rumours that would take the heat off Marsh Barton?' asked Jack.

'Boss, the best we can come up with is that Exeter is Motor City. There are more car retailers in the Marsh Barton square mile than anywhere else in Europe, which means The Hum could be interpreted as road noise. If we pay a bunch of motorcyclists to zoom up and down Bad Homburg Way, round the ring road, and between junctions 30 and 31 on the M5, then we could start a trend, with other bikers and maybe cars joining in. The reason for going with bikers is that they make a lot of noise at high revs, and they can skip past the traffic jams, either in the bike lanes or down the middle of the road. So basically, we need people with a security clearance who can take the trip to Exeter. These people will have to come from USA, or local assets; otherwise, the risk of the Brits finding out is way too high . . . assuming they don't already know,' pointed out Theo.

'All right, that's the first step forward that I can authorise. Make it happen. I want to read about crazy motorbikes in the next issue of *E&E*. And is there anyone we can lean on to make this a daily newspaper again? Once a week is a disaster for us in operational terms,' moaned Jack.

'What about the people on the ground. Have we got names of the ones who responded to our signals?' he continued.

'Boss, so far we've only been able to track people in the Cedars. There is a project underway to wire up Wonford House, in particular the Russell Clinic, which has some long-term mental health patients. Although we've seen a general reaction in the main hospital and out in the community, we don't have the resources to monitor all those places,' said Albert.

'In terms of people in the Cedars, there are two that stand out. Barney has a very explosive temperament and regularly gets locked up in the padded cell, but he seems to be able to discern our signals. He will come out with the names we're sending, in general conversation, so must have heard them in some form. We've not had a chance to interview him, so we don't know whether he's hearing voices or just having words pop into his head. It's a similar story with George; however, he clearly struggles with his symptoms the whole time and talks to his voices continually whilst walking along. He doesn't really engage in conversation with anyone else, but he's the most reliable in terms of coming out with words. The other patients like Star will sometimes react, but they're not at the same level as Barney and George,' said Nicky.

'Do we think that either Barney or George correspond to our strongest receiver signal?' asked Jack.

'That's difficult to say, boss. They're the strongest if you draw the circle around the Cedars, but right now our data don't localise any narrower than Exeter as a whole. So potentially, we're talking outpatients who have already been diagnosed, people who have yet to be diagnosed but have the capability, or other people from outside. We'd need involvement from the Brits to find all people diagnosed with schizophrenia, bipolar disorder, or borderline, who are currently living in Exeter. And as for people who have yet to be diagnosed, we'd have to run into them with a mobile unit to be sure of tracking them down. Right now, our machines are at the scale of a small house or a large industrial unit, so we have some way to go before we can get one in the back of a van,' concluded Theo.

'OK, thanks. Anything else?' asked Jack.

'No, I think that's about it, boss. I'll keep you updated if anything comes up on our ongoing op. And I get the motorbikes out on the roads,' assured Albert.

'Sure. I'll get back to you on whether we want action on any of the other points,' commanded Jack.

Jack walked out of the operations room and into his office and picked up the phone.

'Hi, Malcolm, it's Jack. I've just had a briefing from the team and need to hear your thoughts on a few things. Can I come over?'

'Absolutely, let's do it.'

'So you survived your first briefing then. I'm sure that was enough to give you a headache even with ops based in the UK,' guessed Malcolm.

'Sir, getting straight to the point, I'd like new versions of all of our kit, small enough to fit in the back of a van. Ideally both EM and QE,' stated Jack.

'Of course. It will take some time though,' responded Malcolm, unsurprised.

'I'm arranging another cover story to divert the press and local population. I'll need it if we want to localise further with a longer signal on the strongest-receiver analysis. I assume you're OK with that?'

'Yes.'

'And I'm sticking with B-list celebrities on the send side for the time being. But I want to focus on those that also have mental health disorders. Obviously there's a risk of word getting out, but we can't keep hiding it from the Brits forever.'

'Do it.'

'Permission to approach Barney and George, who are the strongest receivers so far in the Cedars?'

'Granted.'

'Thank you, sir.'

'My pleasure.'

Jack went back into the operations room.

'You've got clearance for B-list celebrities with mental health disorders,' he announced.

'Cool,' said Albert.

'Please approach Barney and George and find out what their experience is,' added Jack.

'Sure thing,' said Albert.

'And when the motorbikes have done their thing, we've got the go-ahead on a longer pulse to localise some more,' finished Jack.

*   *   *

Exeter HQ was located at a house near St James Park in the north of Exeter.

'Hello and welcome. I'm Julia Barnes, in charge of briefing you for today's op.'

'Hi, Julia. I'm Delia Sciuto.'

'And I'm Jeroen Mulder.'

'Pleased to meet you.'

'OK, I assume you've been told very little about today?'

'We're expecting to conduct some interviews and that's about it.'

'Perfect. I'll give you this map of Exeter. We're here and you need to find your way on foot, together, to the Cedars mental hospital on Dryden Road, which is here. It's a secure facility, but you can kick the door down and it will even lock itself afterwards, so basically it's a bit of a joke. Hopefully you won't need to do that and reception will simply let you in and out.'

'We've phoned ahead and they're expecting you. Your cover story is as a couple of reporters doing a story for the *Express and Echo* on mental health. You'll be interviewing Barney and George on Delderfield and Coombehaven Wards, respectively. I suggest you do them one at a time because George in particular doesn't cope with social situations. Whereas Barney is potentially violent so you need to be on your guard with him.'

'Here is a list of general questions, which should hopefully make them feel relaxed. We want you to ask whether they remember hearing or seeing anything associated with this list of keywords—either something that just popped into their head, or hearing a voice, or maybe seeing something. Take your time with this bit because this is what we're really interested in.'

'We believe our location here is secure, so you shouldn't be observed on your way in. However, there is a risk that the Brits are monitoring the Cedars, so we expect you may be followed on the way out. There will be an Apple Taxi waiting outside. Take it to St David's Station. Then get on separate trains, as per these instructions. You'll be staying at hotels for one night. If we think you evaded detection then you'll receive instructions for a follow-on op tomorrow. Otherwise you'll be taking a plane home.'

'Any questions?'

'So we have no contact with the real *Express and Echo* then?'

'No.'

'How do we report back?'

'Don't worry, we've got the place wired.'

'Fair enough.'

At Exeter HQ, Delia and Jeroen left the house on their way to the Cedars. Initial assessment was that they weren't being followed so all was well.

For deniability reasons, Exeter HQ was a minimal secure house set-up, while the main team remained in the US. Local ops were ran from there, including the final go-ahead on EM and QE pulses. Although in the north of the city, HQ was still within EM range so a potential risk for headaches, etc. The last pulse wasn't strong enough to reach that far, but the next one almost certainly would be, if they were operating long enough to gain a fix on the strongest receiver. After that, the decision to remain in HQ or not would be taken. Installation of a Faraday cage was obligatory for the operator in the industrial unit, but would be a complete giveaway in a domestic house.

The secure house on Dryden Road was a much more obvious concern. The QE machine, transported in pieces and then assembled in the front room upstairs, was clearly not something your average house would have. So if cover was blown, then the USA would have a hard time denying it. The two security guards in the room downstairs kept watch of the street 24/7 as part of a rota.

Little did they know that the British Special Air Service or SAS were moving into the house next door.

Meanwhile, back in the USA, Jack was updating Theo.

'Theo, for the next celebrity visit to Dryden Road, whoever it is, I want the QE pulse strength turned up to maximum. That should still be insufficient to affect Exeter HQ, so I want them on observation duty outside, wherever has the clearest view across to Dryden Road.'

'Understood, boss. We will need to up the strength on the EM pulse cover-up as a precaution. If you're happy to accept the risk on that, then I can send these orders over to Exeter HQ.'

'Do it.'

*   *   *

Unknown to the CIA, LJM had met both Barney and George in previous encounters at mental hospitals in Exeter. And his own mental health history was as long as his arm.

LJM's first encounter was in 1998 following the death of his first child. He'd also had a few traumatic events in childhood which probably didn't help either. So the primary diagnosis was for depression, and he was treated with a combination of anti-depressants and cognitive behavioural therapy at the Bucknill Centre in Wonford House.

It was during this time that he met Barney. They got on really well and became friends. However, Barney was not friends at all with any of the centre staff. Suffering from a severe case of borderline personality disorder, he was very emotionally unstable and could flip from being placid to extremely angry in a blink of an eye.

The first time LJM had seen this happen was when Barney was challenged by a staff member. He flew into a rage and two more staff members ran to the scene to help apprehend him. Barney was physically dragged down the corridor and locked into the padded cell.

On another occasion, Barney had a falling out with the staff once more, and they responded by upping his medication to a very high level. He was sat in an armchair in the living room trying to conduct an amicable conversation with another patient, but was falling asleep every twenty seconds, before waking up again with a jolt a few seconds later.

After a while, Barney managed to rack up enough time on good behaviour to be allowed out into the community. He even offered for LJM to come round to his house, and they listened to CDs all afternoon. Barney was as good as gold.

The thing that struck LJM the most was Barney's absolute determination to never give in. If he had a cause to fight for, he would fight to the death. In time, LJM recovered and was released from Wonford House. That was the last he ever saw of Barney.

The next time LJM was admitted to a mental hospital was in 2014. By this time, the centre had moved from Wonford House to the Cedars. He had experienced a period of increasingly manic behaviour and was diagnosed with bipolar disorder (formerly known as manic depressive disorder). It is characterised by intense mood swings from high to low and back again.

Depression is fairly easily managed in most cases, although it can result in suicidal behaviour. Conversely, manic behaviour is much harder to manage, with feelings of invincibility, high levels of alertness, lack of sleep, impulsive behaviour, and scant regard for resources or other people's sensitivities. In extreme cases, it can result in psychotic behaviour with delusions and hallucinations.

In LJM's case, he had a build-up of delusions and at least one hallucination by the time he arrived at Delderfield Ward. In particular, he was paranoid that he was being watched by Security Services and had seen a flash of light, seemingly from the centre of the earth.

During the next two years, he had several more admissions, with both mania and depression. In the most extreme case, he'd started to hear voices in his head. This was regarded as hallucination by the doctors, although interestingly, LJM noted that other cultures such as shamanism regard them as significant.

Either way, the crux of the matter is who judges what is delusional? Defined as a belief in something that is false, what's to say that the patient isn't right and the rest of society wrong? This was the space into which Project Blue Crystal was heading.

LJM was out in the Exeter community when Blue Crystal landed in London. He observed their experiment as a flash of light from the east. This was a bit like being done by a speed camera, except that it was only one flash instead of two. Either way, the experience was enough to put him back in mental hospital.

It was during this time that he met George. George had an acute case of schizophrenia, which basically meant that he experienced psychosis the whole time, whereas with bipolar disorder and others, the psychosis is episodic.

George would walk down the corridors talking to himself the whole time. Actually, he was talking to the voices in his head. If you said hello, you would get a hello back, but that was about as much of a conversation as he could hold.

For LJM, the experience of the Honiton operation was magnified, but he was on the recovery and was out of the Cedars before operations turned up in Exeter.

Delia and Jeroen pressed the buzzer at the Cedars reception. They went with Delderfield first to meet Barney and got the most hostile encounter out of the way first.

When they were admitted to the ward upstairs, Barney was waiting on the purple-coloured seats in the communal area. Ellie the staff nurse introduced them and led them to the Quiet Room.

'Barney, we're here as part of a report being written for the *Express and Echo* on the possible existence of telepathy. We understand that you have borderline personality disorder. Do you mind if we ask you some questions?' asked Delia.

'No, that's fine,' said Barney, visibly relaxed.

'Do you hear voices in your head?'

'Yes.'

'Would you say that these are fantasy or reality?'

'They're real inasmuch as I can definitely hear them. But I change my mind as to whether they represent real people or not.'

'What percentage of the time would you say you believe they're real?'

'Maybe 80 per cent'

'So 80 per cent of the time you effectively believe in telepathy?'

'Yes, I guess you could say that.'

'What advantage does that bring?'

'It brings me lots to think about and new ways of looking at the world. But it comes at the price of being locked up in hospital.'

'We've brought a list of keywords that you may have heard from the voices in your head. Would you mind putting a tick against the ones you remember hearing, please?'

Barney studied the list and did as he was told.

'So in rough terms you've heard around half of these names?'

'Yes, that's about right.'

'Barney, thank you very much for your time. You're free to go now, and we'll continue our survey downstairs.'

They all shook hands, knowing the interview was a hit.

The story with George in Combehaven was a disaster by comparison. His schizophrenia meant he was unable to hold a conversation with Delia or Jeroen and just kept on talking to the voices in his head. In a very short space of time, they concluded that the interview was a miss and left George to his own devices.

*   *   *

It was midday and the motorbikes were starting to turn up on Alphin Brook Road, behind the crowd on Grace Road South. As per instructions, they started to head out along Hennock Road Central and Bad Homburg Way, before turning left around the A379 Ring Road. Occasionally, one would go right as far as Kennford and back again or take the long way round on the A38 and M5.

At 8 p.m., they were given instructions to come into the central part of Marsh Barton to increase the noise and cover for the evening op. Everyone in the St Thomas area could hear them. The crowd was gone by this time.

The op itself was scheduled for 9 p.m. Kingsley Khan, the operator in the industrial unit, was on standby for a call from HQ.

At Dryden Road, two security guards were the only people in the building. As the op didn't involve the QE machine, the decision was taken to run on minimal staff. They would be unaware of what hit them.

Julia was under orders to remain in place at Exeter HQ. She was told that she was far enough north that the risk was minimal.

The EM pulse would send a low-level humming sound, audible to many, but over a long-enough duration to gain an accurate signal and mild enough to avoid any obvious 'simultaneous headaches' reports. They agreed on fifteen minutes. This would of course give the crowd much more to chew on the next day, but the motorbike story was already being sent to *E&E*.

Julia gave the order for Kingsley to go ahead with the pulse. Even from inside the house, upstairs, she could instantly hear it as The Hum and assumed that most of Exeter could too.

She phoned USA HQ straight away.

'Are you nuts? I can hear it loud and clear from here. Minimal risk, my arse. You're gonna have massive crowd tomorrow if you don't pull the plug on this right now.'

Jack thought about it for a moment.

'I hear what you're saying Julia, but it may just be that you're in the 10 per cent that can hear it. We need a clear directional signal on the strongest receiver and this is the only way. After this, we can relegate the EM machine to cover-up duty only on the QE ops. We have a strong cover story in place. Continue.'

Julia hung up and decided to go downstairs. That only served to increase the noise levels.

She went outside and things were much the same out there. Then she made an unusual decision to take her shoes off. She'd heard that being in direct contact with the ground was the way to maximize the signal. And they were right . . .

If it was like this here at St James Park, what was it like in St Thomas? None of the agents had clearance to hang out there during ops because of the minimal risk argument. Julia was about to say 'bollocks' to that and take things into her own hands. She ran to the end of Well Street, up along York Road and onto Sidwell Street in search of a taxi. If she ran all the way to St Thomas, the fifteen minutes would be up by the time she got there.

After five minutes, she found a taxi outside John Lewis. But then calculated that a ten-minute ride in traffic would get her no advantage. So she elected to run after all. In bare feet.

Meanwhile at Dryden Road, one of the security guards was moaning about a headache.

And so were two of the SAS men in the house next door, while a third said he could hear a humming sound. A fourth one went outside and said he could hear motorbikes in the distance. He also suggested that maybe it was the weather.

When Julia got to the intersection of High Street and South Street, she slowed to a walk. She could hear The Hum even louder now, as she continued down Fore Street. And she was convinced that she could hear voices in the distance, in the Cowick Street area. The motorbikes weren't in direct line of sight because of the buildings, so that didn't wash as a cover story with her.

And then it stopped. And so did the voices. The silence was deafening, apart from the distant sound of the motorbikes, which could now just about be heard from where she was.

She felt like phoning again right away, but thought better of it because it would break protocol. She wasn't sure if she had been observed on the way down, but either way, her absence from HQ would be noted.

So she headed back, after putting her shoes back on.

The situation in Dryden Road was much the same. The headaches took a while to dissipate, although the SAS man who heard The Hum said he could no longer do so.

In Hennock Road North, Kingsley was relieved. He congratulated himself for the complete operation. He'd escaped without any harm done, even at point-blank range, thanks to the military grade Faraday Cage he was confined to. He went outside and got some air.

At that point, he discovered the first major cock-up of the evening. The two security guards were unconscious on the ground.

'Oh heck, did nobody think to warn them? I thought that was supposed to be handled by HQ because they sure as hell don't report to me,' he mused out loud.

Kingsley went back inside and phoned USA directly.

'Major problem, two security guards down, please advise.'

Jack took a deep inhale of breath.

'Hell, we forgot the bloody security guards. At that range, yes, they would be toast. Does anybody have any information on what that would actually do to them?'

'Boss, the closest we've ever done a proximity test like that is fifty metres. We assumed that the whole section of Marsh Barton is devoid of people that time of night, so the chance of anyone getting closer than that is remote.'

'And?'

'They spent three days in intensive care but then made a full recovery. That was with a pulse strength 50 per cent of what we've just gone with.'

'So their chances of them making it is remote then. Higher strength pulse, way shorter range, no Faraday Cage, stood on the ground.'

'Please advise,' Kingsley repeated.

'Shoot them. Make it look like a professional hit. Then phone Secure Force UK and let them handle it from there.'

'You've got to be kidding me.'

'Do it. Those are your orders. The security guards won't make it and a shooting is a better cover story than death from The Hum.'

*   *   *

Julia phoned in when she got back to HQ.

'You haven't actually tested this thing on real people have you? You just developed it and put it into operation in a foreign country, causing total chaos in the process. You have no idea what this thing actually does, do you? I tell you, it's obvious from miles away, and I could hear people out of their houses yelling about it too.'

'Julia, we're on the front line hunting for terrorists here. It's imperative we find the strongest receiver before they do. In the wrong hands, this could give them an unthinkable strategic advantage, on the scale of the Enigma machine in World War II. I accept that things can get a bit out of hand, but we're doing what we have to. The other thing to bear in mind is that maybe you didn't hear real voices. Maybe those were caused by you tapping in as a Receiver yourself.'

Julia was stumped at that point. She'd assumed the voices were real because she'd had reliable mental health her whole life. If her head was starting to cave in then that was even more scary than what she'd witnessed.

'I need to know if your role is secure.'

There was a pause.

'It's secure.'

The following morning was practically a riot. There were triple the crowd numbers on Grace Road South, spilling out onto Alphin Brook Road as far as the roundabout and around the entrance to Hennock Road North too.

The motorbikers were stopping and telling crowd members that it was all a joke and that motorbike noise was to blame. They were then putting their helmets back on and zooming off.

Meanwhile, Secure Force UK had phoned the police regarding the incident with the security guards. There were police cars and blue-and-white tape everywhere. Murder was not a regular thing in Exeter, so to have a double contract killing was off the scale.

Kingsley was under orders to cooperate with the police. He was to give them a tour of the building and explain that he was working late. He had his headphones on and certainly didn't hear any of the shots, but he did feel something resembling The Hum, and he wondered if it was coming from the Energy Recovery Facility.

When he gave the tour, there wasn't much to show: a large, mostly empty space with some machinery at one end. He explained that it was a part for the next generation of energy recycling, and he would be taking delivery of the rest of it soon.

Needless to say, Kingsley didn't escape questioning and was detained at Heavitree Police station. He sat in a cell, waiting for the interview team to be assembled.

*   *   *

'Did we get the data download?' asked Jack.

'Yes, boss, we sure did,' answered Theo.

'Cool. So even though we're one EM machine down, with a bit of luck, we'll have a fix on the strongest receiver, and we won't need it again, at least in the short term. We'll just have to take a risk with any QE ops that we don't clean up afterwards and put up with whatever the consequences are. In any case, using it again while the crowd is out in force is just asking for trouble.'

'What about Kingsley, boss?'

'He'll be fine. It doesn't add up that he would shoot them and then phone in, waiting for Secure Force UK to turn up. And we can always extradite him if it comes to it.'

'And what about the EM kit?'

'Leave it. They don't have the information on how to operate it, and they won't know WTH it is.'

'Surely there's a risk they'll equate The Hum with the kit?'

'Maybe. But it won't do them any good because without Kingsley, it won't be firing up again.'

'How long will the data analysis take?'

'Two days, boss.'

'What? Please tell me you're using some decent computers. Or is this running on some 286 museum piece?'

'We have a cryogenically cooled supercomputer from IBM, with some simple interpreted serial code that crunches in matrix format.'

'What's wrong with a massively parallel machine?'

'The lead time on developing the code is way too high. By the time we finished, the next version of the hardware would be out, and we'd have to redo the whole thing again. Not to mention that debugging it is way harder so we'd be forever cautious about our results.'

'So there's no way I can have it today then?'

'No. Sorry, boss.'

A giant exhale of air.

'OK, let me know when you've got it. We'll step up ops with the QE machine for the next couple of days. Then look to relocate to wherever we've got a fix on the strongest receiver.'

'Sure thing, boss.'

INTERROGATIONS

This time there was no escape for David Cameron. He was told about the SAS involvement on Dryden Road, where there could be a terrorist cell operating in the house next door. However, all leads pointed to the USA as the source.

Then there was the double shooting on Hennock Road North. Kingsley, who was an Australian citizen but living for the last few years in the USA, had been detained pending questioning. And there was some suspicion regarding the purpose of the machinery he had assembled in the industrial unit.

Finally, the crowd were out in force again, still blaming the Energy Recovery Facility for The Hum, although there was some suspicion that it could be motorbike noise.

'So what do we do?'

'Question Kingsley first. Then get on the phone to the Americans and ask if they want him back, in return for telling us what the hell he was up to.'

'What about the machinery? Is there no record of where it came from?'

'None, whatsoever, I'm afraid. The only things we have on record are the rental of the unit and the hiring of the security guards. Exeter simply wasn't on our radar back then, so they could have driven it in plain daylight and we'd still be in the dark.'

At this stage, Jack was beginning to realise that he'd made a bad call. The prospect of Kingsley being interviewed by ever more senior police and civil service was not something that had occurred to him. He'd assumed that he would be let go by the local police, and his jibe about being extradited was not so funny if he lost his job over it. Actually, killing the security guards in the first place was on his watch, so he would probably be had up for that too. He knew that Blue Crystal had an extraordinarily high turnover of staff and he was beginning to see why. Julia had only been in the job less than a week, and she was showing signs of going over the edge too.

He walked into Malcolm's office.

'OMG, Jack, what a mess-up.'

'Sir. Leaving the security guards out there was an oversight. I take responsibility for that. However, I wasn't briefed on how lethal the EM machine could be, so it was an easy mistake to make. I felt I didn't have an option in letting out the message that The Hum could kill. So I elected to take a risk with Kingsley for the sake of keeping it under better wraps with the general public. I believe I've acted in the best interests of my country, though I appreciate that this may bring us into conflict with the Brits.'

'It sure as hell will. We're expecting the President to be on a call with the Prime Minister within the hour. Our best sources say that Kingsley will be interviewed first, but we don't know by whom.'

'What should we do in the meantime?'

'Carry on. You're a ruthless bastard, Jack. Just don't kill anyone else.'

'We have a two-day wait for the EM pulse results, which should give us a fix on the strongest receiver. Then I recommend relocating the QE kit and going as far as we can in that direction. Until then, we'll carry on with the experiments at the Cedars. I'd like authorisation to turn that machine up to full power for the next op.'

'Authorised.'

Back in the main project room, USA HQ.

'Theo, please give me full briefing on how the QE set-up works. I need to understand my options.'

'Sure thing. Laura is the expert. She'll bring you up to speed.'

'Boss, the QE machine is delivered in parts and installed in situ. Whereas the EM machine works by sending a pulse into the ground, the QE machine works as an airburst. We generally place it upstairs in a domestic house for cover. This gives us the best line-of sight to the target. The current machine works up to a radius of 800 metres at full power, though so far we have operated within the designated safe range of up to 400 metres.'

'For your next op, Laura, I'd like to operate at full power, 800 metres. Will this be a problem?'

'No, boss. In that case I would recommend an alternative arrangement for all personnel involved. There is no Faraday Cage with the QE machine because it doesn't work that way. In fact, there is no shielding device we know of. Although it had appeared to be safe to operate in the same room, including the celebrity Sender, at full power that's deemed too much of a risk. So the celebrity and any other Senders should be placed outside at a safe distance. Putting them in the front garden is still too close, so on the other side of the road.'

'What about the machine operator?'

'Henning Horlicks will have to be in the same room. That's an unavoidable risk.'

'But we don't think it will kill him?'

'No, nothing like that. Mostly people report weird effects. They rarely get headaches. To tell you the truth, I don't even know why they're so cagey about using it at full power.'

Jack considered this for a moment.

'I'm sure they have their reasons. But I have authorisation, so we're good to go. I want a single Sender this time. Ideally a celebrity with a mental health disorder, but I'll take general B-listers if that's all we can get in time. Place him or her on the grass outside the Cedars, as much as possible in between the machine and the hospital. Make up numbers with agents. Today if possible.'

A gulp was Laura's considered response.

'Julia has local command,' continued Jack.

'Understood, boss.'

Malcolm came into the project room.

'We have some more information. Kingsley has been arrested for the suspected killing of the two security guards. He has the right to a lawyer, but he may waive that right, that's up to him. Send Julia in there as his lawyer, and she can keep us up to speed as to what's going on. This is a disaster, Jack. It would have been better to leave the security guards and get the hell out of there. But we can't change that now,' announced Malcolm.

'We need Julia on the QE ops. Without her, there will be no local chain of command, and we'll have everyone operating independently on orders from HQ directly. That massively increases our exposure if any of the agents are compromised. Also if you have Julia in there, that will tie her to Kingsley loud and clear so if they are onto us for the QE op, they'll know that QE and EM are related,' insisted Jack.

'That's a risk we're going to have to take. Prepare a replacement for Julia as her cover will be blown after this. And prepare replacements for the EM team, including Kingsley. We may have to get both of them out of there as soon as they're out of the police station,' pushed Malcolm.

'Do you really think we can carry on EM ops after all this? And what if they charge Kingsley?'

'Yes, I do, though maybe with mobile kit. It's closer to being ready than I thought. Without the weapon, it won't stick. He said he put it in the molten lead apparatus, so they won't be getting that out in a hurry. Next time you feel like shooting someone, get the bikers to do it. Letting our key man fry over this is madness,' asserted Malcolm.

There was a pause.

'OK, I'll get the message to Julia,' conceded Jack.

'Jack, I've already briefed the QE team so that op will proceed without me. I'll dispense with that phone, so they can't phone me back. That means they should contact you by default, as per protocol. We've already contacted them ahead of time, and they were already in Exeter, so was easy to bring the date forward,' said Julia.

'All right. Get on over to Heavitree Police Station ASAP. We need backup for Kingsley. You're his lawyer.'

'Understood.'

Jack hung up.

Julia made some last minute preparations and phoned Apple taxis. There was no point putting any more agents in front of the police, so she elected to wait fifteen minutes for a local one. It was either that or run, but after last night's exercise she was a little sore, not being used to running barefoot.

Twenty-five minutes later, Julia was pulling up outside the police station. She paid the taxi and walked in through the front door.

'Hi, I'm Julia Barnes. I'm the lawyer for Kingsley Khan.'

'Please wait there, Ms Barnes. I'll check for you.'

The duty policeman disappeared through the door and came back five minutes later.

'Yes, that's fine. I'll show you through to the interview room. The duty sergeant will let you know the charges. And you can wait there while we bring Kingsley down from the cells.'

*   *   *

Meanwhile, under the watchful eyes of the SAS, the team had been assembling at Dryden Road. The two security guards who were already there were joined by three agents. And then the celebrity turned up, which was a total surprise to the onlookers.

The first agent, Henning, went upstairs to prepare the QE machine for operation at full power, 800 metres.

The other two agents, Luke and Albert, explained to the celeb that he would be participating in a thought experiment in the hospital grounds across the road. Henning called down to say that he was ready.

The security guards split up, to cover the team across the road as well as staying in the house. The SAS saw their opportunity, but stayed on hold while they observed what the hell they were up to.

The outdoors team walked across the road, up the driveway to the Cedars and then in between the trees onto the grass, where they were in line-of-sight of the building. Then Luke phoned to say ready and held the line while the first fifteen-second pulse went through.

The SAS men all saw flashes of light and heard a variety of sounds from a hissing noise to a rumbling explosion. They were stunned. They started talking amongst themselves, breaking protocol, but the experience was so way-out-there they just had to talk about it.

'That's enough, lads. I'll call it in.'

The message came back to hold position and wait for the team opposite to head back.

The team on the grass was given the go-ahead. As per instructions, each of them focussed on their primary keyword in their mind, which was their name, and remained alert for anything they saw or heard in response. After a minute, they progressed to their second keyword and so on.

After five minutes, Luke phoned that they were done, and a second QE pulse was sent out, for another fifteen seconds. As they were under the trees, none of them noticed it was starting to rain to the east of hospital grounds, with a lovely vibrant rainbow.

Neither did the SAS see it because they were still disoriented by the QE effects.

'Go, go!'

With that, all five SAS bailed out of the house, two headed for next door while three went across the road.

They were observed by Henning upstairs, and he gave the abort signal to Luke and Albert, just before an explosive device was put through the front window downstairs and the whole house went up in smoke. The security guard was shot dead, while Henning put his hands behind his head and survived by giving himself up.

Luke and Albert ran in the direction of Wonford House. At which point the SAS phoned it in because there was no hope of them catching up on foot. However, they were able to apprehend the celebrity, who was amused by the whole thing and thought this was just the next stage in the process.

*   *   *

'Bollocks, bollocks, and triple bollocks.'

'Boss, word is the SAS were camped out next door all along, so we're completely compromised.'

'Did we get the video footage from the Cedars?'

'Yes, boss. It's being downloaded now.'

'Good, so at least we've got the main part of the results. If we recover Luke and Albert on the run, then we'll get their debriefing too, but we'll have to assume the celebrity feedback is gone. And Henning is a serious liability in their hands because he's been caught at it.'

'All operations in Exeter are on hold pending more information on the fate of Kingsley and Henning.'

'Unless somebody can supply me with some mobile kit to go in the back of a van.'

'Is there anything else I need to be aware of?'

'Boss, some of the bikers reported the onset of rain and a rainbow to coincide with the QE op. Coincidence?'

Jack looked visibly shaken. But knew he had to quash that rumour before it got started.

'It's a coincidence.'

'Sure. I'll send the message back.'

'Boss, we have the results back from the Strongest Signal experiment in Marsh Barton.'

'Keep it simple. What have you found?' said Jack.

'The signal is in the direction of St Thomas. It came through loud and clear. The distance measurement has more of a margin of error though. Our best guess is St Thomas church on Cowick Street.'

'Oh my God.'

'Quite literally.'

'What are we looking at? Talking to heaven? Talking to the church? Talking to someone in the church?'

'We have absolutely no idea. The results from the experiments conducted in the US indicated that real people were responding to our signals. But that was from the Quantum Entanglement side. We never did have a concrete idea on what the electromagnetic results were showing us. We know that EM wipes out QE. And we know there is a strong directional signal which led us to London, Honiton, and then Exeter. We've assumed the strongest signal represents a human receiver, but we don't have any proof of that,' said Theo.

'And we won't know any more until we can carry on with experiments in Exeter. The Brits are onto us big time. They've quarantined both the EM and QE machines. Kingsley and Henning are in their custody. The chances of us sneaking in a new set of kit are remote. Even if we shipped it in piece by piece it would still have to pass customs. It would only take 1 piece to fail and we'd be done for. If we go down the covert route, the only way I can see that working is if the kit is small enough to fit in a Transit Van. Conversely, if we share everything with the Brits then we lost the IPR that belongs to the USA at this point in time. There's no way the President's going to agree to that, given how hot the technology is,' responded Jack.

'There may be a third way, boss. We could collaborate with the Brits, but only give them access to the hardware. We would retain the software here, which include both the set-up generation and the results analysis. That way we would always stay one step ahead of the game and overall control would stay here,' proposed Theo.

'That's a thought. For me, the data analysis was always the Achilles heel of the operation. This is 2016 and it's ridiculous that we have to wait 2 days for the results. However, the fact that it's done here makes it much less likely the Brits will be able to reverse-engineer the whole thing,' responded Jack.

'I agree, boss. The communications to and fro are encrypted to military standards, and even if they cracked that, they'd have a hell of a job understanding what it meant, much less be able to write the generation or analysis software,' encouraged Theo.

'OK, so the best deal is sounding like they get the hardware while we retain the software. But the fact remains that the strongest signal is in Exeter and there's no way the Brits are going to let us do more experiments unless we share the results,' concluded Jack.

'The alternative is we put maximum effort into miniaturising the hardware. Assuming we can smuggle it in of course. But communications with the US would likely be spotted by the Brits. We'd have to include the software with the hardware so the overall results could be hidden in a regular phone call, rather than sending masses of data to-and-fro,' surmised Theo.

'That's Pie-in-the-Sky until we can speed up the data analysis. The current situation with 2 days spent on an IBM supercomputer is totally out of control. And on-site analysis could take months or even years with things as they stand,' asserted Jack. He pondered his options for a while.

'What's the software written in?' he asked.

'Ruby,' replied Theo.

'Ruby, Ruby, Ruby, Ruby,' joked Jack.

'I agree it's not the best choice from a performance point of view,' conceded Theo.

'So presumably you put the emphasis on developer productivity rather than outright software performance?' pushed Jack.

'With an interpreter, the develop-run-debug cycle is a lot quicker,' commented Theo.

'Well I'd say that our priorities have just changed. I want a full review of all algorithms to see what can be sped up. And I want it done in a compiled language that gives full access to all the available hardware,' ruled Jack.

'So not like Java then?' teased Theo.

'I don't want to go from an interpreted to a bytecode-interpreted language. I want to go all the way. And head-hunt the best people on the planet if you need to. Those that are willing to relocate to Exeter would be a bonus too', finished Jack.

'Yes, boss. I'll get right on to it,' promised Theo.

*   *   *

Back at Heavitree police station, Kingsley was told he had a visitor. He was brought down from his cell in handcuffs and then freed to stay in the interview room alone with Julia.

'Kingsley, I'm Julia Barnes. Needless to say, I would prefer to have met you under different circumstances. I'm your lawyer for today at least. Can you give me a brief rundown of what happened?'

Kingsley described the end of the operation, when he had discovered the two security guards outside. He phoned Secure Force UK and then waited for the police to turn up. He gave a statement and was free to go that evening as long as he cooperated with police enquiries. The following morning, he gave a tour of the building and was then arrested when he went outside.

'OK, that sounds fair enough. Is that what you said when you were arrested?'

'Yes'.

'I suggest you just say the same thing when questioned. Saying nothing will make you look worse.'

After five minutes, they were joined by two police officers. One of them was in uniform with tattoos on his arms, while the other was in plain clothes and could have been anybody. They introduced themselves.

'I'm Mark Horne. I'll be conducting the interview today. Also with me is police officer Nigel Newbery from CID.'

'Kingsley, you've been read your rights and you understand the seriousness of the charge. You do not have to say anything, but anything you do say may be referred to in court and used in evidence against you. And I see you have your lawyer with you.'

Kingsley nodded.

'This interview will be recorded. This machine here is used for that purpose. It takes a minute to set up, and I'll do that now.'

Kingsley took a deep breath. He knew that they were partly responsible for the death of those men, but that wasn't the point. He wasn't about to carry the can for the whole of the US operation, so denying his part in it was the obvious thing to do. He had a cover story already prepared.

'Today is Thursday, September 10, 2015. In the room are police officers PC315A Mark Horne and Nigel Newbery CID. Also present are Kingsley Khan, under questioning, and Julia Barnes, his lawyer.'

'Kingsley, you have been arrested for the suspected killing of two security guards on Hennock Road North yesterday evening. Do you have anything to say?'

'The company I work for, based in Australia, specialises in energy from waste recycling. We're setting up a small presence on Marsh Barton in Exeter with a vision to expand nationwide. I arranged the rental of an industrial unit on Hennock Road North, and my company placed a contract with Secure Force UK to supply two security guards 24/7. Our kit is highly specialised, leading edge, and worth protecting. I've taken delivery of the first section, with the rest still to be delivered. This means we're only partly operational at this point in time.'

'Last night, I was working late. I had pizza delivered from Domino's Pizza, if you care to check. I had my headphones for most of the time, while I was entering data via the console. I heard nothing unusual.'

'Around 9:20 p.m., I went outside and thought I could hear a low-level humming sound. And there were a number of motorbikes circulating around Marsh Barton. It was then that I discovered the two security guards on the ground. It looked like they had been the victims of a drive-by shooting. I phoned Secure Force UK and reported that their men were down. And they phoned the police based on the information I'd given them.'

'I waited until the police and Secure Force turned up, followed by goodness knows who. I explained my side of the story and gave them a tour of the premises. I was arrested the following morning.'

'Why didn't you phone the police directly?'

'I've been living in the USA the last few years, so I would have called 911 and got the wrong number.'

'Do you carry a gun?'

'No, that would be against the law in this country.'

'Do you own any weapons?'

'Not in the UK.'

'Was anybody else with you in the building?'

'I was working alone.'

'Do you know the names of the security guards?'

'No. They were on a rota so it was difficult to keep up.'

'How come you ordered three pizzas? Feeling hungry?'

Kingsley paused. 'I was catering for the security guards too. I'm nice like that.'

'Did they eat them?'

'I have no idea.'

'Well, there were only crumbs found at the scene. We'll check via autopsy what their final meal was.'

'About this machine you have installed. Can you describe its operation?'

'No.'

'Is that because you're unable to do so or because you don't wish to cooperate.'

'I can give you a demo if you like.'

There was a long pause.

'OK, we're done. This interview is terminated. Kingsley, you'll be escorted back to your cell while we make our decision. It may go to the Crown Prosecution Service, in which case it could take several hours.'

Kingsley assumed that in this case Crown Prosecution Service probably meant Civil Service, given the fuss surrounding The Hum. If they suspected USA involvement, then it would go all the way.

He waited in his cell.

Then thirty minutes later, he was told he was free to go. He went downstairs to recover his things and was given a briefing by the duty sergeant. The sergeant explained that they didn't have enough evidence to secure a conviction, and he was free to go. However, Kingsley's offer to do a demo was well received, and they would appreciate it if he cooperated by doing that. They already had a team assembled and would follow him to Marsh Barton.

Blimey. This was all a bit too immediate for a local affair, so Kingsley assumed it was already at a national level. They couldn't very well charge him with double murder and then ask him to do a demo from his cell, so presumably that was why he'd been freed.

'I'd like my lawyer to attend.'

'Sure.'

So they all travelled in two police cars to Hennock Road North.

*   *   *

Jack was feeling distinctly uneasy. 'What the hell is Kingsley planning? If we do a full-power demo, as per the current settings, that would take out everyone not sitting in the Faraday Cage. Given there are only three seats, this could be a deadly game of musical chairs. And nothing short of mass murder.'

Theo thought about it and then offered an alternative. 'We could calibrate the EM machine for stun. Doing at the low-level setting for fifteen minutes is clearly way too much. So we could turn it down to say one minute. Or we could go for a higher frequency, which is less audible and more punchy. We would only need say fifteen seconds to disorient everyone in the room and give Kingsley and Julia a chance to escape.'

'OK, that sounds promising. We don't know in advance where everyone will be standing, but even if they're outside they'll still be stunned, right?'

'Yes, that's right. They'd have to get a significant distance away not to be stunned.'

'I'm liking the sound of this. Then we can send in two bikes to pick up Kingsley and Julia. How far away would the bikes have to be?'

'They're insulated on rubber tyres, as long as they don't put their feet down. Likewise, any other cars in Marsh Barton will be fine. It's only pedestrians who will cop it, and there's not so many of those, fewer still on Hennock Road North. We will have a few casualties in neighbouring units, but at a lesser level than the ones in the building.'

'OK, the thing to do is put Kingsley in control. Send him the data for a medium strength, medium frequency EM pulse, and leave it up to him how long he runs it for. Give him your best estimate. And plan a route out of the both of them. Is the main door the only way in or out?'

'Afraid so.'

*   *   *

The police cars arrived at Hennock Road North. Kingsley and Julia emerged with six spectators. They weren't introduced, so Julia assumed they were government agents. She thought one of them may have been the guy she'd seen on TV at the Energy Recovery Facility.

They went into the building, and Kingsley explained that he needed to make a phone call with his company to get data download organised for a demo. Nobody questioned that it would be the middle of the night for an Australian company.

'Kingsley here, with Julia. We're doing a demo to six VIPs. What have you got for me, Jack?'

'We're going to download data for a medium-strength pulse, set for stun. Your call how long you want to run it for. Julia can wait it out in a police car. We'll have two bikes waiting for you outside as a getaway. Understood?' instructed Jack.

'Yes, I'm assuming we'll have the usual ten-minute download?'

'Correct.'

'OK, I'll give a tour first, so expect to be ready for download in five minutes.'

'We're ready. Do it.'

Kingsley hung up.

'Ladies and gentlemen, I'll give you a brief tour of our facilities first, and then I'll set up the machine for a demo. It takes ten minutes unfortunately, so please feel free to talk amongst yourselves or walk outside into the sunshine while I'm doing that.

'My company specialises in energy from waste technology, a bit like the facility in Grace Road South just over there, which has attracted the interest of the crowd. We operate a closed loop system, but as we've only taken delivery of one part so far, I can only demonstrate in open-loop mode.

'The full loop processes energy from waste as well as waste from energy. The idea is that by setting up a feedback loop, we get better overall system efficiency.' This was all complete rubbish, but sounded plausible; hence, why Kingsley was the best man for the job.

'The component you see before you is the waste from energy part. It operates off a standard three-phase supply, storing energy in its coils, waiting to be released when required.' This was true. 'We have a cast lead ground connector. Ideally, we would use gold, silver, or copper, but those are all too expensive for a demo set-up. Lead is a good enough conductor and in plentiful supply from local roofing merchants.'

'Are there any questions?'

'What will we see when you switch it on?'

'You won't see anything but you may hear something.'

'Any hints?'

'It depends on your personal make-up. Different people experience it in a different way.'

There was a pause while Kingsley spoke in a low voice to Julia.

Kingsley then climbed into the Faraday Cage and sat at the console. He got on with his tasks, while Julia took her cue and walked outside to get back in the police car.

Ten minutes later, Kingsley was ready. He climbed down and went outside to round everyone one up.

By the time the last person entered the room, he was in position, ready to go.

He flicked the main control switch and a kind of dark comedy ensued. They all started to randomly move body parts in a weird dance. Clearly, they had lost voluntary control, but Kingsley was sure they would get it back straight away if he turned the machine off, so he carried on. After ten seconds, the last person had fallen to the ground and was convulsing along with the others.

'That's enough, let's go.'

Kingsley flicked the switch off and jumped out of the cage.

'This will keep The Hum rumours going indefinitely. Ouch.'

The people around them started to roll around in a groggy kind of way.

'Quick, this is our chance.'

As per the plan, two bikers were outside with two spare helmets. Kingsley got on one but Julia decided she was happier stealing a police car instead. Just before they sped off, one of the policemen struggled outside. He was composed enough to observe what was going on and phoned it in.

The bikes raced down Bad Homburg Way, then turned left at Matford Roundabout. The escape route was via the ferry at Plymouth, but they didn't want to drive directly there in case they were being followed. So they headed past Exminster towards Kenton, before turning right for Kennford. When they got to Kenn, a car was waiting. Julia was mightily relieved.

Once in the car, which was a black Mercedes, it was a way more comfortable ride, albeit down country lanes to start with.

When they arrived onto the A38, they went up Telegraph Hill to give the impression they were heading for Torquay. Then got off at the junction at the top of the hill and took a right turn through the woods towards Exeter Racecourse.

They popped out onto the A38 again and assumed they were free. They certainly weren't followed, and only a police helicopter would have been able to keep up.

* * *

Jack was feeling like a complete failure at this point. They had killed two security guards and done a demo which would put the EM kit squarely in the frame for The Hum. The only saving grace was that Kingsley and Julia would likely make it out of the country, and that they wouldn't have a clue what The Hum was really all about. Unless Henning talked, of course . . .

GOVERNMENT SHENANIGANS

David Cameron took another briefing on the Exeter situation.

'Sir, we have some more information. Questioning Kingsley Khan didn't reveal anything. We had only circumstantial evidence to hold him, so we let him go on the proviso that he gives a demonstration of his machine to some VIPs. We used the head of the Energy Recovery Facility, two civil servants and a detective as well as the two policemen on duty. Reports are a little hazy after that but it would appear that the machine caused them to go into a kind of nervous breakdown, during which time. Kingsley and his lawyer Julia Barnes made their escape. It seems they had two motorbikes waiting, and they headed south out of the Marsh Barton Trading estate.

'And further to the SAS stake-out on Dryden Road, they've apprehended the machine operator, Henning Horlicks, and a security guard, along with a minor celebrity. One security guard was shot dead when they stormed the house and two of their agents escaped. Reports from the SAS mentioned that the machine has seriously weird effects, causing them to see flashing lights and hear noises. While the celebrity says he was asked to do some simple thought experiments whilst standing on the grass outside the Cedars mental hospital. I know this is sounding like something out of a James Bond movie, but I'm not making it up. The SAS have Henning in an interrogation room. Awaiting your orders.'

'What's the connection with USA? I understand Kingsley has lived there for the last few years and Julia is one of theirs. What about Henning and the other two agents?'

'Sir, Henning is from Canada, while we suspect the other two agents are from the USA. So there is quite a strong connection to the US overall. We haven't been able to trace their phone calls yet, but we suspect the trail will lead back to USA also. We're also starting to investigate the influx of bikers we've seen recently, given their involvement with the escape.'

'So they're not being particularly subtle about it. Which suggests that either they have a lack of local assets or they're in a hurry. Would you agree?'

'Yes, sir, that's a fair assessment.'

'In which case, the real question is, what the hell the Americans think they're doing running terrorist cells on British soil? And why? Do we have any idea what the purpose of these machines is?'

'None, sir. Both would appear to be based on electromagnetic signals of some sort. The one on Hennock Road North sends signals into the ground, judging from the cast conducting plate it's sitting on. Also, the metalwork enclosing the operator would appear to be a Faraday Cage that insulates its occupants from the worst of the signal. Whereas the one on Dryden Road sends signals in all directions, including through the air and walls to affect the SAS soldiers. There is no Faraday Cage with that one, so it must be safer to operate.'

'What's the low-down on the celebrity involvement?'

'It doesn't make any sense to us, sir. It could be just an elaborate cover story.'

'And what on earth are they doing outside a mental hospital, of all places?'

'Again no idea on that one, sir. We can either try to extract some answers from Henning, or you can approach the Americans and ask them directly. Assuming they want Henning back and are prepared to talk.'

'And how will we know we're getting the truth?'

'We won't, sir. This is all unchartered territory. Their machines are clearly cutting-edge technology of some kind. We could take them apart in an effort to reverse-engineer, but that's no guarantee of success and would destroy them. If we want to know more about what they do, we're better off putting Kingsley and Henning back in control, as part of some kind of joint operational agreement with the Americans. But this is all hypothetical without you talking to them first.'

'OK, I think I have had enough. Please get the US president on the line, and I'll take it from there.'

'Barack, this is David. I hope we haven't got you out of bed.'

'Not at all, David. It's a fine morning here. I hope it is where you are too. How can I help?'

'We have comprehensive evidence for two terrorist cells operating in Exeter in south-west England. One on Hennock Road North. One on Dryden Road. In each case, we've apprehended the personnel and taken possession of the machinery they were operating. The purpose of these machines isn't clear, though both appear to be sending electromagnetic signals of some sort—with either weird or very worrying effects. The two key men are Henning Horlicks, who is in our custody, and Kingsley Khan, who has escaped with Julia Barnes, his lawyer. There is a strong US connection with all of this. Please tell me what is going on.'

There was a pause.

'I'm not familiar with those names, but I'll check for you.'

'And you deny any involvement.'

'We're hunting for terrorists, David. You know the score.'

'I can accept that up to a point. But running live operations on UK soil without my say so is absolutely beyond the pale.'

Another pause.

'Let me get back to you after I've had a briefing.'

An exhale of breath.

'Understood.'

Half an hour later.

'David, this is Barack. We've established that Henning Horlicks is Canadian and Kingsley Khan is Australian.'

'And we've traced phone calls from both Kingsley Khan and Henning Horlicks to Julia Barnes, who is American. So please don't pull the wool over my eyes.'

Another pause.

'David, the security level classification for all this is above my level. We could offer to give you a briefing, but unless you've got a PhD in Maxwell-Dirac theory, it won't make any sense to you. And you would become a potential target for the information alone. Send one of your top people to us, to operate out of our headquarters here, and we'll handle it that way.'

'Agreed. But I still need some sort of explanation for why you're here.'

'We're following someone.'

'A terrorist?'

'Potentially.'

'In a mental hospital?'

'Possibly.'

'With some celebrity help?'

'Yes.'

'To say it's weird, doesn't even begin to cover this . . .'

'I can see it sounds like something out of a science fiction novel.'

A final pause.

'OK, I'll get someone lined up and send them over to you. In the meantime, how about you instruct Henning to cooperate with us in return for his freedom. And if you return Kingsley to us in a cooperative mode then we won't press charges either. The kit on our soil remains under our control from here on. If Henning or Kingsley are to run any more ops, they will be reporting to us.'

'Agreed.'

Henning was in an underground basement room, judging from the light, seated at a table, with one other chair and nothing else. He was expecting to be tortured for his information, so was pleasantly surprised when an agent came in with a mobile phone, saying it was his boss on the line.

'Henning, it's Jack. We've done a deal with the Brits. Your cooperation in return for your freedom. If you tell them what you know in a straightforward way, they say they'll release you pending further questioning or operations. If you're involved in any more ops on UK soil, you'll be reporting to them.'

'For how long, sir?'

'That isn't clear. But you can expect to be in the UK while we sort this out.'

'Understood.'

The agent took the phone and went out of the room.

After a while, another agent came in.

'Henning, my name is Chris. Our respective countries have come to an agreement. We're expecting that you're going to cooperate with us by telling us what you know about the operation of the machine in Dryden Road. Then once we're done, you'll be free to go. Can I assume you're on the same page?'

'Yes'.

'OK. Well, in your own words, how about you explain the nature of your operations.'

Henning thought for a moment. If the USA and UK were cooperating, then he may as well take it from the top.

'A few years ago, in a research lab in Canada, a breakthrough was made. Actually there were two breakthroughs at more or less the same time, the other one was in Australia. In the first instance, the Australians discovered that they could significantly increase the conductivity of the ground (i.e. rock) with a particular pattern of waveforms. It was a feedback-driven process, with reflections measured and changes made to the signal accordingly. A bit like homing in on the resonant frequency in every direction, with increasing distance from the source. The effect is not understood by standard science. There are some candidate theories, such as matter separation into positive and negative inertial components. The positive inertial-mass electrons flow in one direction, while the negative ones go the other way. So you get both a positive current and a negative current, a bit like the holes in P-type semiconductors. Anyway, the machine is known as the electromagnetic machine or EM for short.'

'And the one in Canada?'

'We discovered that it was possible to generate a signal that results in huge numbers of entangled pairs. Whereas the Australian machine sent signals into the ground, ours sent signals into the air in all directions. And worked quite happily through walls and windows. This is known as the quantum-entanglement machine or QE for short.'

'So what?'

'The American military showed an interest in both technologies and commissioned some tests. It was during those tests that they discovered some weird results. Basically, if people stood in the way then they would experience a number of different things. These range from hearing sounds and seeing flashes of light, to headaches and nausea. If the EM signal strength is strong enough, then at close range it can cause electric shock, nervous breakdown, and even death. Whereas the QE signal just causes weirdness, so is a lot safer in that regard.

'The really interesting findings came when some subjects reported hearing voices. After further investigation, about half of them had a mental health history. Including schizophrenia, bipolar disorder, or borderline personality disorder. So those people were all in the frame for prior episodes of hearing voices as part of psychosis. Whereas the other half, it was surmised, were all candidates for mental health diagnosis in the future.

'The implication of this was that our QE technology was somehow interacting in the brain's function and causing voices to be heard. If the voices are delusional, as commonly assumed with psychosis, then this would be no big deal. However, if the voices were real, then we had the makings of a telepathy system.

'The other thing, we discovered was that the EM technology returned information on the direction of strongest signal reflection. And with a clever design of signal pattern, it could return distance information too, though with less accuracy. In the case of people, it was often the ones with mental health history that showed the strongest reflection.

'And so was born a programme to deliver working telepathy. In the first instance, the sending and receiving of single words or thoughts. In the second instance, remote hearing. And in the third instance, remote viewing. We're still at the first stage, with scant evidence for the other two.'

'What brings you to Exeter?'

'In telepathic terms, we think in terms of senders and receivers. We're interested in finding both strong senders and strong receivers, so we can work with them to further test our technology. We don't necessarily expect strong senders to also be strong receivers and vice versa. Of course it would be nice to find an all-rounder, but we're not hung up on that.

'From our tests, we believe that people with a mental health record (or potential mental health record) are the strong receivers. Whereas celebrities are strong senders. If we've understood it correctly, their ability to project their message to millions of people also works in telepathic terms.

'We conducted a series of tests in major cities across the USA. And in each case, the result came back that the strongest receiver was in the east, in the direction of the UK, at a distance of 3,000 miles.'

Henning paused. Not sure whether to reveal the ops in other towns in the UK. He chose not to.

'Which brought us to Exeter.'

'So if I've understood this correctly, the EM machine is the one on Hennock Road North. That establishes the strongest receiver signal, but can also electrocute people who are nearby and generates a low-level noise called The Hum by the popular press. While the QE machine is on Dryden Road and that establishes telepathic connections between people who are within range, including the Cedars Mental

Hospital. And also causes random noises and flashes of light, according to reports from SAS.'

'Correct.'

'And what are the results from the operations to date?'

'I don't have visibility of that.'

'So you can't tell me who is the strongest receiver?'

'No.'

'What about the strongest sender?'

'Best guess is Madonna. The number one selling female artist of all time. We haven't worked with A-list celebrities though. They were deemed off-limits. So we've only done B-listers so far.'

'And?'

'No idea. Again I don't have visibility of those results.'

'What about people in the Cedars?'

'Ditto.'

'If we wanted you to demonstrate the QE machine to us, I take it you wouldn't have a problem with that.'

'The pulse data generation is done in USA, so we would have to cooperate with them, as we would for a live operation. Otherwise, no problem.'

'Understood.'

'OK, I'm done. I expect you'll be repeating this a number of times more as they send in additional experts.'

Sigh.

*   *   *

David Cameron was taking yet another briefing from his security advisors.

'The Americans are saying that they want to continue their operations in Exeter. And that they want Kingsley Khan and Henning Horlicks back at the helm.'

'So all of a sudden they've got the good grace to ask, whereas before they were quite happy to sneak around under our noses?' demanded David.

'I guess the fact that we have one of their men in custody and took possession of their kit probably had something to do with it . . .'

'And they want us to turn a blind eye to the blatant electrocution of half a dozen people in Marsh Barton? Not to mention the suspected killing of two security guards? This is getting incredulous.'

'They're saying this is all part of a top-secret military project called Blue Crystal. That the results are of massive security concern and could affect world peace. And that the technological spin-offs could ignite a new bull market.'

'Now it's sounding more like an episode of "Star Trek". The things I'm not hearing are "Why does it have to be Exeter?", "What do their machines actually do?", and "What's in it for us?" Why should we give them an inch after the way they've gone about this so far?'

'They're offering to share results with us. They want to retain the IPR on the machines, but they'll give us a technological briefing to bring us up to speed.'

'And Exeter?'

'Apparently, they're following a signal that one of their machines is giving them. They started in USA and then followed it to London, Honiton, and then Exeter.'

'Are you telling me that they've been doing this in London, and we never noticed?'

'Correct. They only did one electromagnetic experiment, and it told them the signal was 160 miles to the west, which was why they went to Honiton. It seems like their distance measurement is only approximate because they then found out the signal was actually coming from Exeter.'

'And why were they camped outside a mental hospital of all places?'

'They're keeping quiet on that. The debriefing from Henning gave us some clues. It's something to do with the way people respond to the Quantum Entanglement machine.'

'So they have two machines, and they're conducting experiments with both of them at the same time?'

'Yes.'

'What's your advice then?'

'Sir, whatever this technology is, we're lucky that the strongest signal was traced to the UK. Otherwise, we'd never have heard anything about it and wouldn't have any chips to bargain our way onto the table. This way, we can give them what they want in exchange for a heads-up.'

'What exactly do they want?'

'They want to install both machines in St Thomas church on Cowick Street in Exeter. Then conduct some experiments from there.'

'No way. They can have a building nearby, but I'm not giving them a place of worship that has more history than their entire country. And I want full operational control from the UK. They don't get to do a single thing on our soil without asking us. And we sure as hell won't be electrocuting or killing any more people.'

'OK, we'll find a building and report back.'

*   *   *

'So what do you have for us, Albert?' asked Jack.

'I've compiled a report of all the factors leading to St Thomas church on Cowick Street, Exeter. In the first instance, the name St Thomas refers to one of the twelve apostles. Thomas was known as the "doubting Thomas" because he doubted Jesus's resurrection when first told about it. That's interesting because if there is a yang to every yin, then St Thomas represents the opposite view held by the other ten apostles, bearing in mind Judas Iscariot had died by this point.'

'The church was originally built in 1412 and then rebuilt in local sandstone in 1657. Baptisms and burials go back to 1554.

Marriages go back to 1557. It suffered some bomb damage in 1942, but that's about it.'

'The alignment of the church is north-east to south-west. It's not exact, but that's roughly in the direction of Honiton, Andover, Basingstoke, and London.'

'The really interesting find comes when you dig around the subject area a bit. The St Thomas Ley Line runs from London to Exeter. It has the St Thomas hospital in London at one end and St Thomas church in Exeter at the other. So the name Thomas is cropping up rather a lot here. It seems our experiments have simply traced the line from one end to the other, with a minor stop-off in Honiton because we got the distance wrong.'

'Boss, the Brits have come back to us with a proposal. They're offering for us to use a ground floor flat in Buller Court, which is at the far end of the churchyard.'

'How close is it to the church?'

'Around 50 metres.'

'Why not the church itself?'

'They kept going on about a place of worship. Even though it's currently surrounded by scaffolding and building works, they won't let us in.'

'And there's nothing closer?'

'We pushed for the Goa Spice restaurant, which is right next door, but apparently it's a lot easier for them to relocate a few old people and keep a lid on it. They don't trust the restaurant owner basically.'

'OK. We'll tell them that when the results come back and the strongest signal is from the church itself, the President himself will be turning up to start the digging.'

He grinned. 'Will do, boss.'

*   *   *

Over the next week, British security forces took possession of Buller Court. They discussed leaving the other occupants in situ, but then decided it was too much risk to their health, so they moved them to an alternative accommodation. They were told this was a temporary measure while they fixed a radon gas leak in the basement.

They staged some roadworks outside, diverting pedestrians to the other side of the road. Then took a calculated risk with people in the surrounding houses and the Loft Club flats. The police were on hand to cordon off Cowick Street on the pretext of a bomb scare, to minimise the risk to pedestrians and motorists.

The Americans argued that it was important to keep the people in place in case there were strong signals associated with any of them. The British were having none of it though. They wouldn't be conducting any more experiments on real people on their watch.

The Americans took delivery of two new machines, having mothballed the ones at Hennock Road North and Dryden Road. They cast a solid copper conductor plate on the concrete in the ground floor and used that as the basis of the EM machine. Then they put a QE machine in the same room. The place was to start operations with the EM machine and then take it from there.

The Americans assured the British that they would configure the machine for a radius of 100 metres, which meant that the pulse strength would be about twenty times smaller than the Marsh Barton experiment. This would mean that even at close range, the effect would be a mild stun and nothing remotely lethal. However, the British stuck to their guns and insisted that they would be taking no chances.

* * *

'Blue Crystal? What's that all about?' asked David Cameron.

'The EM machine sends signals through rock. Crystals are transparent and made of rock. Blue is a colour associated with communication; hence, Blue Crystal.'

'You're not telling me that legions of people will be going to the crystal shop, coming out with pendulums, divining rods, and goodness knows what?'

'No, we're not expecting that reaction. Although to be fair, none of us understands how this stuff works, so it's worth keeping all lines of investigation open.'

'In that case, I want every scientific test we can think of done in St Thomas church and around the churchyard. And when we're done with that, every pseudoscientific test we can think of. If this strongest signal is real, and it's here in the UK, surely this is a golden opportunity for us to get one step ahead.'

'We may as well start with a radon gas test seeing as that's the cover story. Then we could do some seismic studies, test for magnetic anomalies, and so on.'

'That's the idea. Let's put our top people on it.'

'What priority should I assign to this?'

'Maximum.'

'Are you sure the Americans aren't doing this as some kind of April fool?'

'It's a possibility, but it's quite an elaborate and expensive hoax if that's all it is. We have to assume they're on to something real, and there's a serious upside to whoever gets there first.'

'What if all our tests come back negative?'

'Then we're at the mercy of the Americans for providing more data and doing more experiments. At least we'll have ruled out everything else.'

'If we put our top people on it, then all of a sudden the security clearance goes out the window. Surely we want to keep all this a secret?'

'The Americans are saying it's top-secret military, but there's nothing to stop us spreading the information wider. We haven't signed a contract or anything.'

'This could all go seriously legal if they try to do that.'

'It's a question of what's important. If they want to keep up the pressure on making progress, then they'll have to put up with a less secure operation. If they want to do a deal with the military, then we'll have to give them a whole load of resources to tackle this kind of project. It will end up with the same people involved either way. The top people will float to the top.'

'The best plan is probably to keep it within security services for the time being. Then make it a military project if we need that kind of muscle. There could be some serious crowd control implications if they keep doing experiments on real people. Not to mention what would happen if any of this leaked out.'

'Agreed. Security services can have whatever resources they want to conduct the scientific experiments'

'I'll get them all to sign the Official Secrets Act and make sure we have the only copy of the results.'

'And likewise with the pseudoscientific tests.'

'Are you serious about that? We'll be laughed at by the whole scientific community.'

'It would be a brilliant cover story though. We could leak the story that something weird is going on in St Thomas church. Then we could invite every weirdo in the country to give us their opinion about it.'

'That's like a warped version of the truth.'

'Exactly. The Americans will probably do their nut, which makes it all the more appealing, wouldn't you say?'

'David, it's Barack. I have to say we all think you've completely lost the plot here. The radon gas test was supposed to be the cover story and yet here you are doing it for real. Then what's worse, you go to the press and announce to the whole world that something weird is going on with St Thomas church! You clearly don't understand the security with this project.'

'I disagree. Exeter is only twenty miles from Dartmoor, which is a huge pile of granite rock with associated radon gas concerns. We're only taking due precautions by getting one done in the St Thomas area. And since you didn't supply us with a satisfactory description of what is actually going on with your technology, we're simply being sensible by covering all bases.'

'By getting people with crystal pendulums and divining rods to wander about in the churchyard? You refused access to us and then invite the whole alternative community in through the front door?'

'You were the ones who generated The Hum rumour, which is all over the press. Without telling me. And then you told us about the St Thomas Ley Line. Which is a load of bollocks by the way. There is no such line. Anyway, Ley Lines are made up after the fact by drawing lines on a map that seem to line up with two or three settlements. Anyone can do it. So if we're talking alternative, then you started that too.'

Barack took a deep breath.

'How long are you planning on keeping this up?'

'We're doing pseudoscientific tests first. Followed by scientific tests. Then when we're done, you'll have clearance for your EM experiment in Buller Court. The target is two weeks.'

'I can't emphasise how much imperative there is to move this along. The longer we wait, the more likely the terrorists will pick up some chatter and torture their way into some hard information. Then we've all got a real problem on our hands.'

'If you'd come to us sooner, then you'd be further ahead. Plain and simple.'

'What about the QE experiment?'

'Denied. Live operations on real people are off the agenda. At least until you can demonstrate to us in a series of properly controlled tests what these machines actually do. We're only letting you do the EM experiment as a token of good faith, on the grounds that the local population is cleared out of the way first. And we're trusting you not to electrocute anyone. Unlike what happened in Marsh Barton. My first responsibility is to my people.'

'My people won't accept that. We don't know for sure whether the signals originate with people or places, so it's vital we cover the ground and find out one way or the other.'

'Then you'll have to put maximum effort into the technology demonstrations. We'll set that up as a top-secret military project, at a location to be determined. Probably in the middle of the firing range on Dartmoor, which is as far as you can get from major population around here. We may as well face up to the fact that Exeter will be the new Roswell. The rumours will get out one way or the other.'

'Don't you guys know how to conduct a top-secret project?'

'As long as they don't involve doing experiments on members of the public without their consent, then yes. You can't have it both ways. If you want to do your experiments on the Great British public then we need to be satisfied of their safety. And with plausible deniability.'

Barack took a quick briefing from his staff.

'You're aware that the QE experiment is most effective on people with mental health issues. Your recruitment will have screened that out. So experiments on military personnel will not be representative.'

'Let me take that one away, and I'll get back to you on that.'

There was a pause.

'OK, thanks for your time, David.'

*   *   *

The Home Secretary was in a meeting with the Director General of MI5.

'I'm sure you've heard of this Blue Crystal project the Americans are trying to push our way,' he said.

'If that's their name for it. Our main focus so far has been to bring to an end their terrorist cell operations in Exeter,' she said.

'Good call for putting the SAS on Dryden Road. Apprehending Henning Horlicks red-handed has really put us on the front foot for once.'

'And I hear you eventually caught up with Kingsley Khan and Julia Barnes after a bit of a chase. As far as we can tell, those were the three senior cell members in the UK.'

'From here on, nothing happens on UK soil unless we say so. We're taking a joint approach with the Americans. We're allowing them one EM experiment in Buller Court, next to St Thomas church. Meanwhile the QE machine is off the agenda until they can do a full military handover.'

'Who will you experiment on? Soldiers? I can understand keeping it close for security concerns and the risk of harming anyone. Assuming we can get past that stage, then there is something so be said for widening the audience. I'd want a member of my team in there, so we know what to look for if another one of these blasted things hits our streets.'

'We've got customs watching out for anything similar, but the Americans will get inventive and find a way of sneaking it in somehow.'

'In that case, the QE test results are everything. As soon as we hear reports of anything like that going on then we'll know who to suspect.'

'Is there no way of doing better? This is a major strategic concern.'

'Only if you want to do a press release and scare the hell out of everyone. We're not at war with the Americans yet. But if they continue with covert operations then we rapidly will be.'

'It will be a war of words for now. If the Americans had approached us up-front about a top-secret military project, then we could have responded in kind. As it is, they've left a blazing trail half way across the country and everyone in top-level government knows what's going on. So their secret is not so secret any more. We had to say something in the press as a cover story for the sudden attention in St Thomas church. It wouldn't take them long to join the dots with all of The Hum rumours that were already flying around.'

'So we've changed the cover story from The Hum to pendulums and divining rods?'

'The Hum will rear its ugly head as soon as the EM machine is switched on again. We're prepared for that. But the focus on St Thomas church is not so easy to explain. We thought it would be poetic if we hid behind some new-age fold with Blue Crystals. The story I want out there is that they've discovered something significant with churches around Exeter. Start with St Thomas, then move to the ones in town.'

'How about we open a crystal shop on South Street in Exeter? Then we can promote whatever we want from there.'

'Any chance you could put it opposite American Hair and Nails?'

'That would be a bit in their face seeing as we know it's a safe house of theirs.'

'Even better if you call it Blue Crystal.'

She smiled. 'The Wicked Head shop is still going strong then?'

'And so is Little Witch in Weston-Super-Mare,' he responded.

*   *   *

The Prime Minister sat down in a meeting with the Secretary of State for Defence and the Chief of the Defence Staff.

'I'm sure you've heard the rumours, that our good friends, the Americans have forced a bit of a situation on us.'

'We heard that they've been operating two pieces of untested military hardware in mainland UK. And without your permission, sir.'

'Yes, that's about the size of it. The Americans are claiming a pair of scientific breakthroughs, which clearly gives us an interest in what they're doing. The rub is that they also claim they've been following signals halfway around the globe, with the trail finishing in Exeter of all places. They're fanatic about carrying on, meanwhile we're intent on holding them to account.'

'Surely the thing to do is arrange a full military hand-over for both machines before going any further?'

'I agree. We've outright denied them permission to continue operations with their QE machine until you report back after extensive tests.'

'QE, sir?'

'Quantum Entanglement. The other one is called EM for electromagnetism.'

'And what is the situation with the EM machine?'

'We're allowing them one more controlled experiment in Exeter, under the supervision of MI5 and the local police. In return for some disclosure on the technology and results. After that, we'll go for a full military handover on that machine too.'

'Is there anything I need to know about what these machines do?'

'We'll get the Americans to give you a briefing. The EM machine works by sending signals into the ground, while the QE machine sends signals into the air. And if you stand too close to the EM machine, you can expect to be electrocuted, resulting in either temporary paralysis or death. There's some connection with mental health patients too. That's as much as I know.'

'I assume you'll want us to set up trials in a military base with a secure perimeter, somewhere in the UK. Like Bovington?'

'I've had a discussion about this and we'd prefer to do it on neutral ground, as far as possible from local centres of population. Dartmoor firing range is ideal.'

'You really don't trust them?'

'I don't think they've properly evaluated their own technology. They're just going on a power-crazy trip driven by the latest set of results. It's clear their own military never did any kind of proper handover, or they would have the answers to all of these questions.'

'It will take some logistics to get people and hardware onto Dartmoor. Hikers will notice.'

'Then we can tell them we're doing a confidential joint military exercise. Which also happens to be the truth.'

'Perhaps we could tell them we're doing a radon gas test, sir?' Smiled the Chief of the Defence Staff.

'In the middle of Dartmoor? Let me guess, the results come back as positive that granite produces radon?' joked David.

'What's this I hear about people with pendulums and divining rods in Exeter churchyards?' asked the Secretary of State for Defence.

'Think of it as our very own competitive technology.'

The three men were in hysterics.

*   *   *

'Jack, we've just heard that the British are pushing ahead with military testing on the QE machine. They want to conduct trials at the firing range on north Dartmoor. In UK terms, that's about as far as they can get from local people,' said Malcolm.

'They're not taking any chances, are they? What about Wi-Fi in a place like that?'

'I think we'll get laughed off if we tell them that our cutting-edge military technology doesn't work without a Wi-Fi connection.'

'That's the truth of it though,' said Jack.

'The truth is also that it's madness for Henning to be on the front line. He's the one who invented the technology, though thankfully the British don't seem to have cottoned onto that.'

'Yes, but that was part of the deal we had with Henning when we took delivery of his technology in the first place. He couldn't explain it in any kind of way that was satisfactory to our science team. So instead he offered to put himself on the field as a guarantee of its safety, in return for the opportunity to push ahead and get new results.'

'Well now, we're doing a handover to the British, maybe it's a good time to get Henning back. He's a scientist, not a soldier.'

'I agree. And so do our own military. They're fully on board with the approach the British are taking. They say they would have done a full handover and testing if they'd been given the chance, rather than being steam-rollered by Congress.'

'It seems this technology bestows absolute power on whoever is at the helm. And as we know, absolute power corrupts absolutely,' said Malcolm.

'Henning and Kingsley have stayed on target. And Kingsley has the death of two security guards on his conscience. I know he'll claim they didn't report to him. But he'll know that if he'd lodged an objection, they'd still be alive. He's a soldier now. Though I'd support him returning to science too.'

'We have two problems to solve then. First, get Henning (and Kingsley when his time comes) to do an operational handover to the British so they're not on the front line any more. Second, remove the dependence on a Wi-Fi connection. Presumably by stuffing a van full of computing hardware and sending it to the UK.'

'And I'll guarantee you that they won't like the fact that the operator can't even control the signal strength. The whole thing is done in software, which actually puts Theo in the position of absolute power. All the operator does is to switch it on and off.'

'And even if we ship him in a van to Dartmoor, that will still be the case. Also he covers both machines. We need to split this up so that we have two different people in charge of the software side for EM and QE.'

'What about the processing of the results? Surely we need to retain that here so we have a firm grip on the IPR. Otherwise, we'll be giving the whole thing away.'

'Hardware manufacture stays here. And results processing stays here. The operational side can be completely delegated.'

'Hypothesis, method, results, conclusion. If the method and results are under joint military control between us and the British, then that leaves the hypothesis and conclusions to the scientists. Like it or not, Henning and Kingsley are still going to have overall power over this thing,' said Jack.

'Only until such time as we come up with an explanation for what's actually going on. Maybe those guys don't really know how it works either, and they just got lucky.'

'Which is why the British are taking the piss out of us with pendulums and divining rods. A new age explanation is better than no explanation at all.'

There was a pause.

'All of this is going to take time.'

'Which means they have no choice but to get Wi-Fi onto Dartmoor.'

'Or a very long Ethernet cable . . .'

TRIO UNLEASHED

Julia, Henning, and Kingsley were granted some time off while operations were on hold. Curiosity got the better of them though, and they decided to check out Exeter some more, starting with the Blue Crystal shop they'd heard about on South Street.

'Hi, I'm Julia.'

'Pleased to meet you, Julia. I'm Alice. How can I help?'

'I see you have a lovely new shop here. Is there a demand for this sort of thing in Exeter then?'

'There are crystal shops in many towns throughout the south-west. Exeter already has a traditional one on Gandy Street. We've decided to cater for the upcoming interest in scientific investigations.'

'Scientific investigations?'

'Yes, we get a lot of demand for crystal wands and pendulums, and we also stock rods for divining purposes. It's become very popular in and around churches, with many people reporting strong signals.'

'That's fascinating. What about Blue Crystal then?'

'Blue is the colour of the throat chakra, and so is associated with clear communication. In the past, people used to think about lines of force, lines of energy, Ley Lines and so on. It seems the modern focus on communication has revolutionised the field with some startling results.'

Kingsley and Henning looked at each other.

Julia ignored them and carried on. 'If I wanted something in Blue Crystal then, what would you recommend?'

'Well, you can choose between fluorite, topaz, aqua aura quartz, or angelite. We're going to be expanding the range in the next couple of weeks because of the popularity, so do check in again.'

Julia picked up a large quartz pendulum and marvelled at it.

Henning picked up a fluorite wand. 'What does this do?'

'That's a wand. You can use it to amplify your energy. It's particularly good for healing purposes.'

Henning raised his eyes to the ceiling, at which point Julia trod on his toe.

'They're lovely. Presents are on me. I'll have the pendulum please. Henning, you can have your wand and Kingsley, you can have a divining rod.'

Kingsley thought better of looking at the ceiling, so he looked at his shoes instead.

'Which churches do you recommend?'

'Well, there's the Gothic Cathedral of course, with Norman towers. The oldest church is St Olaves on Fore Street. That's reputed to be a Viking church and predates even the Norman invasion.'

'What does the latest gossip say?'

Alice frowned a little at this point. 'There was an article in the *Express and Echo* last week which focussed on St Thomas church on Cowick Street. The participants in that survey reported stronger signals from the Baptist church on the other side. And the Spiritualist church on York Road, needless to say.'

Julia smiled. 'Needless to say.'

When they got out of the shop, they all played with their new items.

'Is she for real? This has got to be a government set-up. A shop called Blue Crystal suddenly turns up in Exeter,' observed Henning.

'I bet you haven't had this much fun in years,' countered Julia.

'So what's next?' asked Kingsley. It seemed Julia was still very much in charge.

'I thought I would just pop over the road and get my hair and nails done. Then we can have lunch and decide on the route for our local history tour.'

Kingsley and Henning looked at each other once more.

'Are you sure you wouldn't rather go hand-bag shopping instead?' teased Kingsley.

'Come on, mate. I spotted a news agent around the corner. I'll buy you a copy of *New Scientist*, while we wait.'

'Let's see if I can find the way with my divining rod . . .'

Towards the end of their lunch, at 7 Wok, the Chinese restaurant on Palace Gate, they'd more or less come to an agreement on their route. Up the hill for a brief look at the cathedral, followed by a visit to the way more interesting sounding St Olaves. Then a walk down the hill for a visit to the biblical St Thomas, assuming the British would let them in. They could live without the Spiritualist church, particularly since it was reputed to be a more modern building.

'So who exactly was St Olave?' asked Henning. 'I've never heard of him.'

'I'm one step ahead of you there,' said Julia. 'King Olaf of Norway converted to Christianity. Then being the good Christian that he now was, he decided to convert as many other people as possible. So he had churches built in his name and turned himself into a saint in the process.'

'What's the Viking connection to Exeter?'

'They invaded multiple times. In 1001 and 1003 for a start, St Olaves church is dated to around 1045. That's way old, for any church in England.

'And then the Normans invaded in 1066 so it was all changed again.'

'King Harold's mother, Gytha, survived. She was of Viking descent, and we think the church was built for her.'

'Blimey, that's a lot of history focussed on one place.'

'Yes. Exeter was one of the last places to hold out against William the Conqueror. That's why they built Rougemont Castle, to watch over the local inhabitants.'

'So this business of them being loyal to the crown is complete rubbish then?'

'It depends on which crown you're talking about. They seem to be loyal to the incumbent and hostile to the invaders.'

Kingsley got up to pay the bill.

'You can claim that on expenses if you like,' said Julia.

'For real? It was only twenty-one pounds.'

'We'll be doing things a little differently from here on. You're still reporting to me but working together in an office rather than separately in industrial units and safe houses.'

Both Henning and Kingsley blinked.

'What about operations?' asked Henning.

'You each have one last hands-on demo to do. But we'll organise a handover as part of the deal.'

'And on an ongoing basis?'

'We still want your input on planning the route forward and analysing results. Henning will have visibility of the EM side, and Kingsley will have visibility of the QE side. You'll be working together.'

'So we're expecting to be in Exeter for a while then?'

'I think you can safely say that. You might want to start planning your lives accordingly.'

'Where is the office then?'

'It's at Kings Wharf on the Quayside. That's a Grade II listed warehouse building, above the Waterfront Restaurant. I'll take you down there after we've done the St Thomas visit. It's all within walking distance.'

Kingsley came back with a mint for each of them, and together they walked out of the restaurant and up Bear Street towards the cathedral. It was a bright sunny day.

They stood outside the west front for a while, looking at the wall of statues. Then they walked around the side to take a look at the towers.

'The towers are Norman, dating from 1114 and would have been built with a much plainer nave. Then a massive re-engineering job converted to a Gothic nave by 1400. It doesn't look it from here, but the towers are twice the height of the ceiling inside.'

They then went back to the main entrance and prepared to go inside.

'Julia, I hate to say this, but it seems disrespectful to go using a divining rod in here,' said Kingsley.

Henning put his crystal wand into his ear.

'I agree. How about we light two candles for the security guards instead?' said Julia.

Kingsley looked pale for a moment, and Henning looked quizzical.

'Sure,' said Kingsley and they walked inside.

*   *   *

The trio arrived at St Olaves Church and took a look from outside first.

'I'll hand it to you, this place really does look old,' commented Henning, gazing up at the tower.

They went inside, and for some reason felt a whole lot more relaxed in there compared to the Cathedral.

Henning stuffed his wand up his nose, and Kingsley used his divining rod as an extension of his trousers.

'So how much Viking blood is there in the local population then?'

'About 2 per cent, I think,' said Julia.

'Will any of them be coming at us with halberds and big spiky helmets?' asked Henning, pointedly.

Julia thought about that one before responding.

'That I can't guarantee. But we have maximum resources and in a fast-moving industry like this, staying one step ahead of the game is the best way to be.'

'Maximum resources?'

'You can have a car each. We'll be staying in hotels for the time being, so I can't promise houses, at least not yet.'

'I'll take a motorbike,' said Kingsley.

'I'll have an Aston,' said Henning.

'You'd better go shopping together on Marsh Barton then. Tomorrow sounds like a good day. Then you can report to me on Monday.'

'Is any day really a rest day?' sighed Kingsley.

'This is 24/7. I thought you'd be used to it by now.'

When they arrived on Cowick Street, they took a look at the churchyard from the outside first. They walked as far as Buller Court, opposite Tesco's before turning round.

'Chocolate?' offered Julia.

'Do we get that on expenses too?'

'If I were you, I'd stop worrying about who was paying for anything.'

'Can I have a Tesco's Clubcard that gives me unlimited spending power then?' mused Henning.

'We'll have three for £1.20. That's a good deal, isn't it?' ignored Julia.

After that, they walked back as far as Goa Spice.

'Looks like a nice restaurant,' observed Kingsley.

'Shall we have dinner there later?' said Julia.

'Cool,' said Henning. 'Shame about the scaffolding on the church.'

They walked down the alleyway to Church Road, then up Tin lane as far as the Loft Club with the amazing mosaic.

'There are three or four of these in Exeter,' said Julia.

'We walked past one under the railway bridge,' commented Kingsley.

Then they walked back to the churchyard entrance, past the church and under the trees.

'Yew and pine, I'd say,' said Henning.

'You know better than me. Shall we go divining?' Julia wandered off, with her Blue Crystal pendulum leading the way. In public, Kingsley felt a whole lot less comfortable messing around, so he elected to use his divining rod in the proper fashion. Meanwhile. Henning used his wand a bit like a light saber.

They met up at the entrance to the church.

'So this is Ground Zero then?' said Kingsley, at which point they all turned round to find their photo being taken.

'Getting married? We haven't passed a law on threesomes yet.'

'And you are?'

'A reporter. *Express and Echo*. We're running a story. I see you've been to Blue Crystal already.'

It was Henning's turn to look pale.

When they were back out in the sunshine, Kingsley wanted to know some more about the handover.

'So which government are we working for now?'

'You don't need to know.'

'And who will I be handing over to?'

Julia paused for a moment.

'Tania. She's a British military officer.'

'And what about my handover?' asked Henning.

'I don't have those details at the moment. There's been a bit of a delay.'

*   *   *

David Cameron picked up the phone to Barack Obama.

'Barack, it's David. I won't beat about the bush. We're pushing out the delivery date for the Dartmoor demo on the QE machine.'

'David, you don't seem to be on the same page as us. You can't mess around with this stuff. Every day is a day when we could lose one of our top people to terrorist attack or worse. What exactly is the problem?'

'There are birds nesting on the firing range.'

'Don't tell me, it's the wrong kind of snow?'

'No, there really are birds nesting on the firing range. It happens every year, and we keep hikers out of the area too. I have to look after the birds too.'

'Well, pick somewhere else then!'

'Like the Nevada desert?'

'Don't kid around. We've already done that.'

'Kill anyone?'

'No. It's fair to say we've not seen the same scale of the results you've had.'

'Which is precisely my point. We're taking delivery of some hardware with unknown specification and unknown potential. In the interests of keeping the kill list to an absolute minimum, we are going to be doing these tests as far from the general public as possible.'

'Do you have any good news for me?'

'We're pressing ahead with the tests in St Thomas. The radon gas test has come back negative. And we're doing a seismic survey now.'

'What about the pendulums and divining rods?'

'Ongoing.'

'Are we allowed to kill any of them?'

David looked horrified.

'It was a joke, right?'

Henning was already in the taxi when Kingsley got inside.

'Sleep well?' asked Kingsley.

'Not too bad, thanks. What do you make of that reporter yesterday? The real thing or another government agent?' replied Henning.

'I have absolutely no idea. The number of coincidences seems way too high to be completely random though.'

'And is Blue Crystal British or American?'

'It was Canadian and Australian when we started. I'm sure it will be Chinese and Russian by the time we're done.'

'And who does Julia report to?'

'I'm guessing she's a double agent now. Which means none of us know where we stand.'

'Better enjoy the ride then.'

'Quite. Can you take us to Bridge Motorcycles please?' he asked the taxi driver.

*   *   *

'I'd like to buy one today please.'

The sales assistant frowned.

'Any particular one?'

'Brand new. What would you recommend?'

'Are you into racing bikes or easy riders? What's your level of experience, sir?'

'I had a few bikes back in Oz. That was a while ago, but I'd say I still have what it takes. Mid range. I don't want to go killing myself just yet.'

'Something like the Honda CBR 500 then?'

'Sounds ideal. Where are we looking?'

'In the shop across the road, sir'

'Ah, yes. Well spotted.'

Kingsley could practically hear him muttering 'Muppet' under his breath.

A short while later, Kingsley came out with a complete set of riding leather, two helmets, and a shiny new bike.

'Is this a good idea?' asked Henning, a little nervously.

'Sure. I'll take you as far as the Aston Martin garage.'

'No wheelies, right?'

'Relax. I'll go real easy on the throttle.'

'How did you pay for it?'

'Finance.'

'We'll have to see if I can pull off the same trick then.'

They pulled up at Jaguar/Aston Martin and Henning climbed off.

'Can you keep the helmet for now? I need to go for a ride in the zone.'

Henning thought about this for a moment and decided to walk into the garage dressed as The Stig. He waved goodbye and said no more.

Kingsley decided to head out of town by turning towards Matford Roundabout. He was getting used to the feel of the bike by the time he got to the Carriages Hotel, where he turned right onto the A379.

With a couple of dual carriageway sections, he was starting to pick up speed and joined the A38 with the intention of heading towards Plymouth. He used maximum acceleration up Haldon Hill and flew past everything else on the road before hitting low cloud and poor visibility at the top.

The twisty downhill section was a breeze, and he decided to do a U-turn at the Chudleigh junction. The twisty section was even better uphill until he entered the poor visibility again, at which point he glanced to the left and saw the American Bar and Grill. For a moment, he lost focus and picked up a bit of a tank slapper. He recovered quickly and noted the diner as a definite place on the shortlist for eating out.

*   *   *

When they arrived at Kings Wharf on Monday morning, Henning and Kingsley took the lift together up to the third floor.

'Not a bad view, is it?'

'From here it's great. Shame about the gallery office though. We could do with some windows out front.'

'There's got to be a limit on what they can pull off at zero notice. I'd be sympathetic,' said Kingsley.

'I'll have a word with Mother Earth. If you don't ask, you don't get.'

'Morning, Julia.'

'Morning gentlemen. How was Sunday? I see you've brought your helmets.'

'Kingsley had a nice bike ride. Whereas I got told I couldn't have a test drive in an Aston Martin. I have to start small and work up to big apparently. I've booked a test drive in a Jaguar for Tuesday at midday.'

'That sounds lovely. You could take us out for lunch.'

'What's the agenda for today then?'

'You have a desk each. Then when you're ready, grab a coffee and we'll have a debrief in the meeting room.'

'Modularic Media. What's that all about?' asked Henning.

'It's a cover story, duh,' said Julia.

'I'm sure we could come up with a better company name than that. If this is Viking territory, and we're the invaders then we need a tribal name of some sort.'

'How about Mongol Mania?' said Julia.

'Military Muppets?' suggested Kingsley. Julia glared at him.

'This is a lot of space for just the three of us,' observed Henning.

'There will be others, very soon,' said Julia.

'I expect they'll want windows.' It was Henning's turn to be glared at this time.

'I'd like you both to sign this please.' Henning and Kingsley took their copies of the Official Secrets Act.

'So we really are in the UK then. What's in it for us?'

'You get these.' Julia handed over two British Army uniforms.

'I didn't come halfway round the world for a dressing up box. What's the deal?' countered Kingsley, irritably.

'Your handover to Lieutenant Tania Orion is on Wednesday. Your rank will be officer cadet effective immediately. You give them some training. You get some training in return.'

'So I'm being offered a position in the British Army?'

'If you complete your training, yes.'

'I'm 40 years old. If they put me through the obstacle course at Sandhurst, I'd most likely break a shoulder.'

'I'm sure they'll make allowances,' said Julia seriously.

'Jesus, I'm going to have to think about this.'

'The British won't operate your machine on their soil without a full handover. And neither will they let you carry on putting yourself on the front line. You're too valuable for that. You both are.'

'What will I do?'

'Everything you're doing now. Just with someone else pushing the buttons. The Royal Artillery has expressed an interest.'

'They like the idea of electrocuting people, presumably.'

'We're all interested in the science. But this is way too dangerous to be charging around in the open anymore. It has to be under military control. This is the full handover you always said you wanted. And part of your exit strategy, if you want it.'

'And if I don't want it?'

'You can do the handover on Wednesday, which will let the British conduct the experiment we wanted to do in St Thomas. After that, you can hand back the uniform. But you have to sign regardless.'

'And if I won't sign?'

'Then walk away. Leaving an international stalemate. And all of your power and control will be gone.'

'Nothing like being over a barrel,' said Henning.

'Henning, your participation on Wednesday is purely as an observer. You'll escort Kingsley to Buller Court and wait while he does the handover to Lieutenant Orion. Then you will both walk back as far as the police cordon.'

'No Faraday Cage for us then,' said Henning.

'Boot's on the other foot now,' said Julia.

'Better get the settings right then,' said Kingsley.

'One more thing,' said Julia. 'Once you've signed the document, I'd like a full briefing on what your machines actually do.'

'You haven't said anything about my handover yet,' said Henning.

'The venue has yet to be arranged. It's fair to say your machine is doing everyone's head in at the moment.'

'And who is my interested customer?'

'Too early to say.'

Both Henning and Kingsley elected to sign. Henning wanted a Navy uniform instead but Julia had run out of humour by this point.

They took the opportunity to grab another coffee before walking back inside.

'Officer Cadet Khan, what can you tell us about your machine?'

'Well, a number of years ago, in collaboration with Henning, I was looking for a new way of sending electrical current through the ground. I was working with Maxwell-Dirac wave descriptions, experimenting with pulsed signals. By continuously retuning the frequency, and listening for reflections in an iterative process, I found I could overcome electrical resistance and massively improve conductivity with minimal power. We're not 100 per cent sure on why it works, but it does. One possible explanation is a phase separation in the current, split into positive and negative parts. This represents traditional positive current on the way out and negative current on the way back. At the particle level, this could correspond to electrons with positive and negative inertial mass, consistent with an article I'd seen originally on *Science Daily*,' said Kingsley.

'That sounds impressive, but can you give us an executive summary?' said Julia.

'I found a way of sending lightning through solid rock.'

'Which electrocutes anyone within range?'

'As a side effect, yes. At longer distances, people experience it as The Hum.'

'And the benefit of that is what, exactly?'

'To our surprise, by analysing the reflections, we found a consistent directional signal. A bit like a radar or a submarine ping. It led us from mainland USA to here.'

'And what do you expect to find here?'

'We're not entirely sure. Henning's work demonstrated psychological effects with a slightly different but related technology. It's possible that we're looking for a person. Or perhaps a geographic location.'

'So what's special about St Thomas church?'

'I have absolutely no idea. That's where the signal appears to lead us.'

'Is it fair to say that your machine is a glorified divining rod?'

Kingsley looked a bit rattled but then composed himself.

'Yes, I guess you could say that.'

'Once you've done your handover, will we be able to operate it for future experiments?'

'As long as you cooperate with the USA for settings generation and results analysis, yes. They own that now.'

'What about taking delivery of new hardware?'

'Again that belongs to them. Any new developments, I offer to them first as part of the deal.'

'Blue Crystal. What's that all about?'

'That's higher than your security clearance.'

'Thank you, Kingsley. That covers it for now. Henning, can you provide a similar synopsis?' said Julia.

'Sure. Whereas Kingsley was working with ground currents, I was looking for airborne effects at the quantum level. I found a way of generating massive numbers of entangled pairs within a given radius, again using minimal power. I was looking for possible communication effects due to wave-function collapse.'

'What's the connection with mental health patients?'

'We noticed that we were experiencing psychological effects when the patients stood within range. Sounds, flashes of light, sometimes individual words. One of our team was particularly sensitive, and we put that down to a known diagnosis of bipolar disorder. It stands to reason that if there is an effect, some people will be more sensitive than others, and we were intrigued to find out why. So we conducted further experiments.'

'On the general public? Without their consent?'

'By invitation initially. When we satisfied ourselves that there was a real effect and that it was safe, we approached the Americans for possible interest.'

'And what was their interest?'

'They split the analysis into Senders and Receivers and the search led them to public figures as Senders, with psychosis sufferers confirmed as Receivers.'

'So you found a way of controlling remotely mental health patients, using celebrities as the bait?'

'You could put it that way.'

'And the health benefits of this are what exactly?'

Henning shrugged.

'What gives you the right to experiment on the general public in the UK?'

'I'm following orders.'

'As part of a top-secret American military project called Blue Crystal?'

'That's classified.'

'Is there anything else your machine does that we need to be aware of?'

'That's classified.'

'Are there any other variants of your machine that you haven't told us about?'

'That's classified.'

There was a frustrated pause.

'OK, that'll do for now. Thank you, Henning,' said Julia.

Kingsley and Henning elected to go outside and get some air. They encountered an employee of one of the other firms in the building, smoking a cigarette in the upstairs car park.

*   *   *

Henning was standing in the car park, again passing the time of day, when Kingsley arrived back with his helmet, followed a few moments later by Julia in a Smart Car. Henning walked over to take a look.

'Fun for two?' said Henning.

'A bit like Kingsley's bike then,' replied Julia. 'If you're into that sort of thing. I much prefer cars myself. So you're not up for pillion passenger today?'

'I think Kingsley wants a ride in the zone. Is that right, mate?'

'You got it.'

'No offence, but going as far as the Aston Martin garage, hanging onto the back, was just about OK. Further than that? No thanks.'

'We're in agreement on something then,' said Julia.

'Is yours a company car then?' asked Henning.

'Might be,' said Julia, cryptically.

'How did you pay for it, if you don't mind me asking?'

'That's classified.'

They went back inside.

'Julia, if we're done, I'd like to go out for a couple hours on my shiny new bike.'

'Sure. Where are you headed?'

'I thought I'd check out Moretonhampstead to Tavistock and back. It's an epic bit of road apparently. Right across the middle of Dartmoor.'

Julia raised her eyebrows, wondering if he'd heard anything about the proposed experiment there. If he had a higher security clearance, then it was entirely possible, but meant he'd most likely broken with protocol and contacted USA directly.

'Enjoy,' she said. 'I'll most likely go shopping myself.'

'Barack, it's David. Is there anything you're not telling us about your machines? We're all getting very twitchy here.'

'You have everything you need to know,' replied Barack.

There was a pause.

'We're going ahead with the EM handover to the Royal Artillery in St Thomas tomorrow. Right now, we don't have a clear customer for the QE machine, though.'

'You don't have a Minister for Telepathy, then?' jibed Barack.

'Funnily enough, no.'

'Then invite a load of candidates to the demo. That should spark some interest. Are you still planning on Dartmoor?'

'Yes. I guess we may as well get the Royal Artillery to take it for now.'

'And the birds on the firing range?'

'The RSPB have advised they'll be gone by the end of the week.'

'Woohoo. Thanks for moving it along,' said Barack.

'We'll send transport to Dryden Road. Can you supply people to dismantle the QE machine? We'll reassemble, assuming it's the reverse process.'

'Agreed.'

*   *   *

On Wednesday, a military transport turned up at Kings Wharf to pick up Kingsley and Henning. They were both very quiet in their military uniforms.

They were escorted to Buller Court, behind a police cordon. They went inside and Tania was waiting.

Kingsley explained how to operate the machine, and Tania was all ears. Then he went back outside with Henning, retreating to a safe distance, or so they thought, at the edge of the cordon.

They could tell when the machine had been started from the low humming sound. The crowd picked it up instantly and started talking about it.

Everyone assumed that the only person in close proximity was Lieutenant Orion, protected by the Faraday cage. Little did they realise that there was one person left in the Loft Club flats, the building next door to the rear.

Henning and Kingsley were escorted back when the experiment was done, without drama.

THEO ENTERS THE FRAY

At lunchtime, Henning went to Bridge Motorcycles and bought a helmet for Julia. He wrote the word 'Panic' on the front, and all the people in the shop thought that he was mad.

When he got back to the office, he placed it on Julia's desk. Then he went to Kingsley's desk and wrote 'Power' on his helmet. Finally, he wrote 'Control' on his own helmet.

When she returned from lunch, at least Julia saw the funny side of it. 'I want Power and Control but you delivered me Panic instead!' she exclaimed.

'You'll have to do a deal with one of us then,' said Henning, seriously.

Theo then walked into the Exeter office.

'Hey, how's our head of software doing?' asked Henning.

'I'm good, thanks,' responded Theo, looking quizzically at the Power, Control, and Panic helmets on the three desks.

'I'm the biker. These two are just messing around,' asserted Kingsley.

'I'm Julia Barnes,' offered Julia.

'Theofanes Raptor. Pleased to meet you,' replied Theo, shaking her hand.

'So do I need to go for a ride with you before I get a helmet too?' asked Theo, noting that Power was on Kingsley's desk.

'I'll take you out later, mate, if you like,' offered Kingsley.

'I guess you'll need to choose between Control and Panic.'

'I really don't like the Panic label so by all means take that one,' suggested Julia, hopefully.

'What have you done to my software?' asked Henning, changing the subject.

'It's not your software anymore, mate. I've got both you and Kingsley by the balls really. To answer your question, we're rewriting the whole thing from scratch. Running a calculation of this complexity in Ruby is a joke. It takes forever, even on a supercomputer,' answered Theo, pointedly.

'So what are you using instead? FORTRAN?' asked Kingsley.

'You've been spending too much time in Met Office land if you think I'm going to do that,' said Theo.

'So what exactly is your plan?' Henning started to look pale.

'We're going for C++. It gives us the best mix of developer productivity and outright performance. We can scale it to a variety of hardware using OpenMP, BLAS, vector processing, matrix operations, parallel computing, the works,' said Theo.

'The rest of the development team will be arriving shortly. They'll be filling up the rest of the office. We decided to relocate the entire team for the benefit of having Henning and Kingsley on hand while we do the rewrite,' said Julia.

'Exciting times,' concluded Henning.

*   *   *

Theo and Kingsley returned from their bike ride with a fresh white helmet in hand.

'Who's in charge of allocating labels then?' asked Theo.

'That will be Henning,' responded Julia.

Henning walked over to Theo, ceremoniously took the helmet from him and wrote the word 'Balance' on the front. 'Use this one wisely,' he advised.

'This is all sounding very deep and meaningful. What's it all about?' asked Theo.

'Have you ever watched *Top Gear*?' asked Henning, rhetorically.

'You'll be familiar with the Stig character then. I have a working theory that there are mini-Stigs walking around inside his helmet, any one of which can take charge at any given time. When he puts his foot on the accelerator, that's Power. When he applies the brakes, that's Control. At the moment he takes his foot off the gas, that's Balance. Opening the door, causing the ABS to kick in or using the ejector seat are all Panic,' he continued.

'This is sounding really interesting,' said Julia. She was feeling a lot happier about being the manager of a world-class team of people with ABS on hand. 'Do go on. How did you come up with all this?'

'If you study psychiatry, you'll know that people suffer with a variety of mental illnesses. Actually, these just represent extremes. Depression is Control, mania is Power, and neurosis is Panic. Another way of looking at them is Past, Present, and Future. Have you read the *Power of Now* by Eckhart Tolle? I hope to write my own book in a similar vein called the *Wisdom of Balance*.

Julia, Kingsley, and Theo all looked stunned and glanced at the labels on their helmets. Theo walked back to his desk.

Julia and Henning went into the boardroom for a one-on-one meeting.

'So what do I have to do to wrestle Power away from Kingsley?' she asked.

'Climb on the back of his motorcycle and swap helmets while he isn't looking?' he suggested.

She smiled. 'And what about taking Control from you?'

'I'm married,' he pointed out.

'I'm aware of that, Henning. I wasn't proposing to hop into bed with you. I was just wondering if you could give me any pointers?' she replied.

'You could always try offering me a deal,' he emphasised.

'Well that's good because that's precisely what I wanted to talk to you about. The British are unsure of the military value of your machine, even though they'll be testing it on North Dartmoor with you in a Navy uniform. The NHS has expressed an interest based on pure research though. They have taken the view that there are too few females in this office, so they're proposing to give you a sex change in return for your machine.'

Henning turned a whole lot whiter than his usual shade of pale. 'Please tell me this is a joke, Julia.'

She smiled once more, happy to have got the better of possibly the most intelligent man on the planet. 'I made up the bit about the sex change. The rest is authentic.'

'What sort of role would I have?' he asked, suddenly feeling much better.

'You'll be a consultant working out of this office on secondment to the NHS. And your machine will be out there somewhere, most likely on NHS grounds. Is that enough of a picture?' she painted.

'Sounds good,' he replied, optimistically.

On Wednesday, when it was time for Henning to have his test drive, they all got into an Apple taxi.

'Are we all going to fit in this Jaguar then? Surely, the sales guy will want to come along too?' queried Theo.

'Leave that to me,' commanded Julia.

When they arrived, Henning went inside while the others stood admiring the shiny new cars on the forecourt.

'Seriously, Julia, I don't mind ducking out if you have any trouble pulling this off,' suggested Kingsley.

Julia gave one of her knowing smiles.

When Henning and the salesman Jeff came out, they all walked across to the car and got inside. Henning familiarised himself with the controls and thanked Jeff for his assistance.

'One of you will need to either get out or squeeze into the back to make room for me,' said Jeff, a little uneasily.

'I'm Julia Barnes, CIA' she said, waving her badge in his direction. Kingsley raised his eyebrows and Henning looked confused.

'You don't have jurisdiction here,' tried Jeff.

'If you contact your senior management, I think you'll find that I do,' she said, giving Henning a nudge.

Henning took his cue and they sped off out of the garage. 'Where are we going, team?' he asked.

'How about the American diner at the top of Haldon Hill? I'll give you directions,' said Kingsley, easily taking up the reins.

Henning enjoyed driving the Jaguar and reasoned that a four-seat car was a good idea if both Kingsley and Julia were effectively in two-seaters.

They all enjoyed lunch at the Bar and Grill, courtesy of Julia and her mysterious expense account.

When they got back to the Grange Jaguar/Aston Martin, they were greeted by a bit of an international incident. The police were there, and Jeff had been joined by his manager Gordon, waiting for them to return to the forecourt.

'Henning, what are you playing at?' complained Gordon, loudly. 'The police are here to charge you with vehicle theft.'

'Relax, I'll buy the car,' said Henning, coolly.

'Sir, that's not the point. You broke the garage terms and conditions for a test drive. You're under arrest for theft,' said the first policeman.

'No, he's not,' countered Julia. 'I'm Julia Barnes, MI5.'

The second policeman took a look at Julia's badge and indicated that Henning should be set free.

'Apologies, miss, we were told you were CIA.'

'I can't imagine where you got that idea from,' she replied, poker-faced.

Kingsley and Theo could barely contain their laughter.

*   *   *

That evening, Henning felt like going for a drive on his own. Having gone west at lunchtime, he decided to go North. He turned out of the car park and onto Topsham Road, then carried on up South Street, round the one-way system, across the Iron Bridge and up-river past Exeter St Davids in the direction of Tiverton.

He was delighted by the car's handling through the twisty wooded section between Cowley Bridge and Stoke Canon. Then on the way out of the village, he steered into the right-hand lane to take the uphill bend at speed, only to be frustrated by the 30 mph limit on the way into Rewe.

After that, he decided to take a more leisurely approach to the ups and downs between Silverton, Thorverton, and Bickleigh.

He crossed the River Exe at Bickleigh bridge and decided to take a different route back by heading towards Crediton. However, he ran into a thick fog on the hilly ground and decided to go back. He ended up back at the Fisherman's Cot for a Pepsi.

In the office the next day, Kingsley thought he would challenge what was going on. 'Julia, I don't get it. You clearly work for an international company called Security Services R Us. You probably have a budget to rival NASA, then of all the cars you could possibly choose, you go for a Smart Car.'

'I can put my shopping on the passenger's seat. What more does a girl need?' she teased.

'Seriously?' he countered.

'Things are not always what they seem,' she said mysteriously.

Kingsley thought about it for a bit. 'You don't actually have a budget do you? This whole thing is running on vapour, and you actually had to go and buy a car yourself. Probably on finance, just like me. Hence the economy.'

'Now, who's a Smarty Pants?' she scored, happy to have the measure of Kingsley too.

Julia mused for a bit and then decided to take a different tack for the rest of the day. 'Henning, are you OK to take us all on a bit of a daytrip in your gorgeous new Jaguar?'

'Yes, sure,' he responded, not knowing what was coming next.

'In that case, I suggest we all go uptown to Mountain Warehouse to get some hiking boots, and then you can take us to Dartmoor for a bit of fun,' she explained.

'Dartmoor is a big place. I should know because I rode across it the other day. Did you have anywhere specific in mind?' queried Kingsley.

'Yes, Tor,' she said simply.

'Why?' asked Theo.

'Because it's the highest point in south-west England, and it also happens to be close to the location where the British military are going to take delivery of Henning's machine,' she expanded.

'Cool,' said Henning.

Once they'd gone shopping, taken the A30 past Okehampton, parked at Meldon Reservoir, and started to clamber on to the moor, their spirits lifted. It took a good hour to get up onto Yes Tor, by which time the sunshine had broken free from the clouds.

'What a view,' said Henning.

'It's absolutely stunning,' conceded Theo.

'What a biblical place to conduct an experiment,' said Kingsley.

'I'm sure it would make more sense to bring your machine up here,' said Henning. 'The whole area is one huge mass of moist granite, and you couldn't get a better ground conductor than that.'

'Exactly.' Kingsley grinned, with fire in his eyes.

For the first time, Julia started to get seriously nervous about who she was dealing with and was wondering if that was the true meaning of her panic helmet.

*   *   *

The following day was an early start. Henning and Kingsley donned Navy uniforms, while Julia and Theo remained in civilian clothes as observers from a safe distance. Henning had thought that Julia would ask for the use of his car once more, but was pleasantly surprised when a military transport arrived to take them to the moors. They took a different route, past Okehampton camp and were driven to the high ground near the firing range, via a bumpy track.

The journey was unremarkable, but the tension in the cabin was measurable.

Julia and Theo were dropped off when they got past the Tors, while Henning and Kingsley proceeded to the destination.

When they got there, the scene was like something out of a WWII movie. Henning's machine had been assembled in the middle, running off a portable generator. They'd agreed on the same preprogrammed settings as before, so there was no need to download the software from the internet.

There was a single row of people that stood to attention in a circle around the machine, which made Henning think of Stonehenge. He noted that half the people were in military uniform while the other half were in white lab coats. If this was an experiment, then they were taking it seriously.

Both Henning and Kingsley were escorted by armed guard, then Henning explained the operating instructions to Tania.

She would be the sole person at the centre of the circle once Henning, Kingsley, and the armed guards had retreated to a safe distance, with the other people in the circle.

Henning thought this was all a bit over the top, seeing as he'd conducted multiple experiments himself from point-blank range with minimal side effects. At least they were being careful.

Once they'd taken their positions in the circle, Tania pressed Go. Without exception, everyone reacted in one way or another. Tania herself let out a loud OMG while others held their heads, muttered WTH and so on.

Henning saw the usual flashes of light and random background sounds. Kingsley did too, but this was the first time for him.

Once the effects had subsided, Henning and Kingsley were escorted away while the remaining personnel were led away for a debriefing.

'David, it's Barack. Can I assume that now you've taken delivery of the Horlicks machine that you'll be moving forwards with it?'

'Barack, I have to be honest. We're all a bit confused by this situation. It appears to have random psychological effects, and it depends on who you are as to what you see or hear. Our test results indicate that mental health patients are the most sensitive, as you suggested. However, if they were seeing hallucinations and hearing voices anyway, then what's the message?'

'David, we're happy for you to carry on experimenting. Henning, the inventor, is available for consultation. Our entire software team is at your disposal if you need firmware-level modifications, and we're considering delivering new hardware to you as and when it becomes available. You're looking for evidence of telepathy.'

'Barack, are you serious?'

'Absolutely, David.'

'And there's nothing else I need to know?'

'No, that's all,' lied Barack.

*　　*　　*

Jack was still reeling from the loss of Theo and the entire software team from his department, but was doing his best to shrug it off.

'Team, the bottom line is that we've sold the QE machine to the British on a general story of telepathy. This means we've lost our ability to use it in the hunt for strongest senders and Receivers. Henning is still with us but on secondment from the NHS. This means we need to focus a hundred per cent on Kingsley's EM machine as the way forwards. The British are taking operational control of that too, but we're optimistic that they'll carry on using it in the St Thomas area,' he announced.

'Boss, without Henning's QE machine, we've lost our ability to tie our signals to individual people. How can we hope to progress on the Senders and Receivers front, which was the whole point of Blue Crystal?' asked Albert.

'The best we can hope for in the short term is to see something in the EM results. Longer term, we hope to get some combined mobile kit in the back of a van that we can smuggle into Exeter. It will be hard getting past their security, now that they're on the alert, but if we leave it awhile, our chances should improve,' stated Jack.

'David, it's Barack. The results from the Buller Court experiment are clear. They show a strong signal in the direction of St Thomas church, at a distance which places the source in the middle of the nave.'

'Barack, are you having me on?'

'No, this is deadly serious, David. It sounds very spooky, I know, but this is real.'

'So now you want me to rip apart the church in the hunt for this signal?' quipped David.

'We've thought long and hard about this, and we've come up with what we think is a sympathetic way forwards. If you can lift some of the floor tiles and then cast a solid silver plate, we can bolt the Khan machine onto that. Then we run the experiment once more and share the results, as we're doing now,' continued Barack.

'And what do you expect to find?' asked David, incredulously.

'We have absolutely no idea. This is cutting-edge research,' concluded Barack.

In the Exeter office, Julia approached Kingsley's desk. 'Kingsley, I'm not trying to come onto you, but would you care to take me for a ride on your bike?'

Kingsley thought about it for a moment and rapidly surmised that Julia probably wanted a private chat and didn't want the British to hear. Presumably, the office was bugged as part of whatever international deal had been struck.

'Sure,' he said, picking up his helmet.

Julia then picked up Henning's helmet with a knowing nod and nothing more was said until they got to the car park.

'So where are we going, boss?' he asked.

'I thought you could take me along the coast road to Teignmouth. You can claim the petrol on expenses,' she grinned.

They headed off and Kingsley rode carefully, knowing that Julia was nervous on the back of his bike, and this may well have been her first time. They enjoyed the view past Exminster, Kenton, Starcross, Cockwood, Dawlish Warren, and Dawlish. When they got to Teignmouth, he pulled up in one of the parking spaces along the seafront.

They pulled off helmets. 'What's the venue?' he asked.

'There's a pub called the Endeavour just along here,' she gestured.

When they got inside, Julia bought drinks, and they sat at a table in the corner.

'Kingsley, I won't mince my words. You come across as a bit of a power-crazy mad scientist intent on blowing up the world. If you ever conduct a high-power experiment on Dartmoor, you'll terrify everyone,' she posited.

Kingsley shrugged.

'The reason we're here is that USA HQ have contacted me with the results of the Buller Court experiment. Apparently, they show a clear signal in the direction of the church, with a number of lesser signals that can just about be seen above the noise. They want to know if these could be People or Places,' she continued.

'The bottom line is we won't know without lining up the people in a circle around the machine and electrocuting all of them,' he said, knowing that would play into Julia's fears.

'Do we really need to go that far?' she pushed.

'If we don't, then the best we can do is to repeat experiments on the end of each signal. The trouble is that experimental procedure requires us to move people out of the way first, so all we will ever find are more signals pointing to more places,' he reasoned.

'I'll give you the results document when we're back in the office. I'd be grateful if you could spend whatever time you need to give us your best analysis. And please take Henning along with you. I need Theo to maintain focus on the software from here on. The rest of the team are arriving today,' she explained.

'My pleasure. Cheers, Julia,' he said, raising his glass.

'Cheers to you too, Kingsley. I should thank you for the steer about budget too. I've been stuck horse-trading for a while on this one,' she raised.

*   *   *

'David, it's Barack. One more thing that I need to add to the list of requests is a dossier on the mental health records of everyone in a 400-meter radius of St Thomas church. I realise this goes against the grain of privacy laws, but we're keen on using the knowledge to better protect the local population in forthcoming experiments.'

'Surely that won't make any difference if we're clearing the area first?' pointed out David.

'David, we want you to conduct the St Thomas church experiment without a security cordon. We'll send you revised settings for a low-power 400-meter maximum pulse. We can always crank up the power and bring in Security for a second experiment, depending on the results from the first.'

'You don't ask for much, do you? Is there any British law you don't want to break?' David sighed.

'I wouldn't ask if it wasn't important. This could be a gold mine for all of us,' speculated Barack.

HENNING HAS SECOND THOUGHTS

Julia sat in the boardroom with Kingsley and Henning.

'Gentlemen, thank you for your insights on the Buller Court results. We seem to be getting this international show on the road. The British have agreed to put Kingsley's machine in St Thomas church on a solid silver conductor plate. They've also agreed to a low-power with the local population in place, so we stand a chance of telling whether the secondary signals represent People or Places,' she expanded.

'We're going up in the world,' observed Henning.

'We're breaking multiple laws to achieve it but hey-ho,' countered Julia.

'You'll need me to do another handover to Lieutenant Orion if you want me to change the settings,' indicated Kingsley.

'Precisely. And if you get it wrong, both you and Henning will be electrocuted. I think you can assume that the British will be getting you to put your balls on the line every time we do one of these from here on.' Julia shivered. She realised in that moment, she'd taken Power away from Kingsley and effectively became the terrorist herself.

Kingsley was cool with the whole thing. Henning was visibly more nervous, but he realised he was trapped and had to trust his colleague not to screw it up.

'How far away do we get to stand?' asked Henning.

'In the churchyard. They'll have graves freshly dug for you.' Julia smiled.

'That's not funny,' retorted Henning.

'Of course not. I'm sorry gentlemen,' she backed down.

The British staged a military funeral in St Thomas church as their cover story. Henning and Kingsley were instructed to turn up in Army uniforms and were picked up by military transport from Kings Wharf as before. Julia had to stand down for this one.

When they arrived at the church, they were shown inside. 'Shame we didn't bring our crystal wand and divining rod,' muttered Henning.

Kingsley chuckled.

'Good morning, Lieutenant Orion,' he said.

'Good morning, Officer-Cadet Khan,' she replied.

'And this is Officer-Cadet Horlicks,' he added.

'Pleased to meet you,' she saluted. They all knew this was a bit of a farce because technically she outranked all of them, yet she was the one receiving training.

'This will take about five minutes for me to show you the software download process.

The settings have been pre-prepared by the software team and are ready to go. Can I assume you have internet connectivity?' he instructed.

'You can,' she replied, loving the power trip.

Kingsley spent the next few minutes going through the details while Henning waited.

'Thank you, gentlemen,' intervened one of the armed guards. 'I'll escort you outside.'

With that, they were photographed by a reporter waiting outside the door. 'I'm sure I've seen you guys some place before,' she said. As usual, Henning was the one who was perturbed.

They walked to their allotted place in the churchyard and waited while the military cleared the area of remaining people, closing the church door behind them.

They could tell when Tania pressed Go because they all received a moderate electric shock through their feet. Kingsley was sure the effect for the local inhabitants would be milder still, unlike last time. The effect lasted twenty seconds, which was as long as they needed to get a decent fix on any signals.

When they were done, Kingsley and Henning were simply escorted away and back to Kings Wharf. Not a word was spoken. They knew that this was more efficient than scaring everyone with huge security. However, the thought that laws were being broken by experimenting on people without their consent started to weigh on Henning's mind.

Julia spotted the sombre mood as soon as they walked into the office. Rather than pushing for information, she decided to come up with one of her alternative plans.

'Henning, would you be up for driving the three of us to Exmouth? I thought that maybe spending some time walking on the beach might be a good idea, under the circumstances,' she requested.

Henning knew that he was cornered once more but agreed without complaint. They changed out of their uniforms and met up in the car park.

The drive to Exmouth was straightforward. Turn right onto Topsham Road, keep going through Countess Wear roundabout, turn left at Topsham over the railway crossing, past Dart's farm, right at the George and Dragon and then carry on for a few miles past Exton and Lympstone. Henning parked at Orcombe Point, and they all got out.

Characteristically, Julia decided to go barefoot on the sand while the men kept their shoes on.

After a while, Henning and Julia were walking together and Henning started to talk, once Kingsley was out of earshot.

'Julia, I'm not happy with this,' he said.

'I know,' she replied.

'No disrespect to my colleague, but his experiment has nothing to do with me. I don't mind analysing results and helping to chart a way forward. But the decision to conduct live experiments on the general public is not mine,' he went on.

'I'll do what I can to get you off the front line. I can see what effect this is having on you. It does mean that you and Kingsley will be taking different paths from here on. Are you still happy to take the lead on your experiment?' she queried.

'I must admit I hadn't really thought about the legal and consent aspects until now. Maybe receiving an electric shock has helped focus my mind. At least the British seem to have the upper hand with my machine, and they're taking a very cautious approach. I applaud that,' he finalised.

'Understood,' she noted.

When they got the results back they were very interesting. They showed a complete lack of a strong signal directed within the church and instead were a number of weaker signals radiating outwards in all directions. The strongest of these was pointing at number 30 Sanford Place.

'That's quite illuminating. It shows that the strong signal towards the church is almost certainly geographical, while the signal towards the house could be either geographical or biological,' said Kingsley.

'I agree. The question is, "What are you proposing to do next?"' challenged Henning.

'I'd say dig up the street. We can't exactly invade someone's home unless we have their explicit say-so. That way we can start to show a separation between the signals and hopefully get a stronger or even a split fix on the house,' suggested Kingsley.

Henning was pleased to see that his colleague at least had some limits, though he was happy to keep on experimenting come what way.

*   *   *

There was quite a buzz in USA HQ, and Jack was called into Malcolm's office.

'We've got him. There's a man who lives at number 30. He has an extensive mental health history with both bipolar and borderline personality disorder diagnoses. We're convinced he must be the strongest receiver we've been after all along,' said Malcolm.

'And what about the geographical signal in the church?' asked Jack.

'Nobody has the faintest idea what that was all about, not even Kingsley,' replied Malcolm.

'Well, Kingsley is suggesting we dig up the street to get a better fix. Should we still go ahead with that?' asked Jack, once more.

'As long as we know that the man is inside then yes. He seems to wear a tan-coloured leather jacket whenever he goes outside, so you'll spot him a mile off. And put a sniper in there. And send Nicky to the Exeter office to assemble a psychological profile,' insisted Malcolm.

'Jesus, boss. Are you sure you want to shoot potentially the most valuable man on earth?' demanded Jack.

'No, but we can't afford to lose him in the general population. If he goes to work and comes back home as normal then fine, but if it looks like he's taking a hike then we put an end to it. Do I make myself clear?' overruled Malcolm.

'Sure thing. Shouldn't we also mount a ground operation to have him followed?' continued Jack.

'At this point we don't have the resources in place to track him night and day. And with the Brits on maximum alert, we're not going to get near him,' pointed out Malcolm.

'So the Brits don't know we're on him?' queried Jack.

'No. And his identity doesn't leave this room. From now on, he'll be known as the Leather Jacket Man or LJM,' finished Malcolm.

When news of LJM hit the Exeter office, Julia decided to keep it to herself. Being boss of a multi-national corporation was kind of fun and rewarding in its own way, but she missed front-line action, particularly when they wouldn't even let her be an observer during an experiment. So she turned herself into a foot soldier once more. As it happens, she was sat at her desk reading a copy of the *Express and Echo* when Nicky arrived.

'Hi, I'm Nicky Alexander,' she said.

'Pleased to meet you, I'm Julia Barnes,' she replied.

'I'm here to do a psych profile on LJM. Is there anything I need to know?' asked Nicky, cutting to the chase with immediate effect.

'I'm one step ahead of you there. How about you take a seat in the meeting room, and I'll be right with you,' responded Julia.

Nicky made herself comfortable.

'I've been tracking LJM for the last twenty-four hours. He lives at 30 Sanford Place, and he works right here in this building,' delivered Julia.

'Are you kidding? How spooky is that?' said Nicky in astonishment.

'He does a nine to five in the software company right across the stairwell,' said Julia, almost as incredulously herself.

'Can I get sight of him? It will help me a lot to see what he's like,' asked Nicky.

'Our orders are to maintain a distance of twenty paces, unless we happen to bump into him in this building.

'How about you walk with me, and we'll stalk him home together?' laughed Julia.

'It's a deal,' said Nicky.

When it came to home time, Nicky and Julia went down for a 'cigarette break' outside the glass-fronted elevator.

'I need to get surveillance organised so we know when he's leaving. You can appreciate how hard that is as part of a covert operation in a country like Britain,' said Julia.

Nicky nodded.

They waited half an hour, and sure enough LJM came out of the building on schedule. He smiled when he caught their eyes, and Julia instantly regretted her plan because she knew she would get a roasting from USA HQ if they ever found out. As long as LJM didn't turn around though, they'd be OK.

This evening it was a nice walk across Cricklepit Bridge, along the river, past the Harvester, across the dual carriageway, behind Marks & Spencer and past the library. As they approached Sanford Place, something completely unexpected happened. A bomb exploded in the churchyard. *Boom*!

Apart from ringing in their ears, Julia and Nicky were unharmed. Julia checked to make sure that LJM was still on his feet before they turned back.

'OMG, we've got a mole,' she said to Nicky.

Back in the office, Julia took an urgent phone call from Jack. 'I assume the two of you are OK,' he stated.

'Yes,' replied Julia.

'We've got satellite observation lined up and a sniper moving in,' he continued.

'How did we miss the explosion?' asked Julia.

'No idea as yet. Either we've been compromised or the Brits are on us, and MI5 is playing hardball,' said Jack.

'I have an MI5 badge, and they try to bomb me. What's that all about?' she demanded, conscious that half of the conversation could be heard via any bugs in the office, assuming that they weren't tapping into the entire phone call.

'I know it sounds daft but it's plausible. You'll just have to wait this one out until we have more information,' said Jack encouragingly.

'I think I'll hope for terrorism. I'm more comfortable with that as an explanation,' said Julia.

The next day Julia picked up the latest copy of *E&E*, noting that it had reverted to a daily newspaper. It was full of speculation about the bombing, military funeral, Buller Court ground operation, and The Hum.

'What did you think of LJM?' she asked.

'He seems completely normal to me. Nothing I've seen is suspicious, but then we've hardly got anything to go on,' she replied.

Julia could see that bringing Nicky to Exeter was probably a mistake. She'd announced LJM as a target in what was probably a bugged room, which meant that the British knew that they were trailing him. It wouldn't take them long to put two and two together based on his mental health dossier.

In reality, MI5 were way farther ahead than the CIA could have imagined. They were able to employ some leading-edge techniques of their own and without the Americans spotting what was going on. Admittedly, the resourcing situation in Exeter massively favoured MI5.

LJM took one of three routes to work. He would go under the railway bridge behind Marks & Spencer, across the junction on Alphington Road, and then along the west side of the River Exe to Cricklepit Bridge. Or he could go under the railway bridge on Cowick Street, across Exe Bridge on the north side, and then along the river on the east side. Or he could go for a combination of the two, crossing Exe Bridge on the south side.

On the whole, he would just walk to work directly and without anything eventful happening. Every now and again though, he would be persuaded to go one way or the other because there was a pretty lady walking that way. He wasn't 'stalking' her as such because he would simply carry on his way. However, there was no mistaking the fact that he would enjoy the view for as long as she was in front.

He didn't have a particular type. Any hair colour, reasonably dressed, and average build would catch his eye. That said, he was a bit of a sucker for particularly well-dressed ladies and those with curvy hips and hour-glass figures.

All of this meant he was a prime candidate for being led on by MI5. He was completely unaware of what they were doing. Placing roadworks in his way, organising crowd of people outside the library so he was forced to cross to the other side, and, of course, strategically placing women for him to follow.

As time passed, LJM started noticing things. Messages seemed to be planted everywhere, specifically for him. Adverts on billboards, shop signs, TV adverts, even vans had familiar-sounding names and slogans. When he went into the supermarket, he was bamboozled with choice and came out with a set of groceries that were pre-programmed, not the ones he really wanted.

On one occasion, LJM went into M&S for some food on the way home. He came out with a bag of basic items and some Purple Grape Juice. After tea, he wandered over to Tesco's for a chocolate bar and encountered a lorry with Welch written on the cab. Welch is the manufacturer of Purple Grape Juice.

The number of coincidences intensified. When he went to the Bernaville Garden Centre in Cowley, it was closed for the bank holiday. He was about to turn back onto the road when two cars arrived at the exact same time from opposite directions. They did a kind of stunt-car manoeuvre, driving around him and then disappearing off into the distance, leaving LJM stunned.

The net effect of this was that LJM became paranoid. He'd seen Derren Brown on TV and was aware of the techniques he used to lead people on. It was as if Derren was controlling his entire world. However, the sheer scale of the operation made him convinced that it had to be the Government.

To cope with the stress, LJM's mind split into two separate identities, one which believed that the messages were real and another that did not. The different identities also represented different personalities that he could adopt. By this time, LJM was on the borderline of psychosis, unable to tell the difference between *fantasy* and *reality*. In effect, MI5 were driving him mad, and he was only vaguely aware of that via the paranoia.

All of this meant that LJM was extremely vulnerable. MI5 could plant a strong message, and it would have an almost immediate effect. For example, an AA Refuel van was parked outside the Sawyer's Arms, causing him to go out and refuel his Land Rover that evening.

It got to the point where LJM thought that the TV was talking to him personally. Not just adverts but subliminal messages and even targeted remarks from game show hosts like Alexander Armstrong. On that occasion, LJM felt that he was being instructed to walk up into town. MI5 were waiting with a string of women to lead him on this way or that and with scenarios invented to test his abilities. At the end of the operation, he bought some groceries in the Co-Op on Fore

Street and then arranged on the ground near St Edmunds church ruins, in a kind of motif message to the heavens. In short, LJM was in a state of total confusion, and this was precisely what MI5 wanted to bring on psychosis, hearing voices, and seeing hallucinations.

Their working theory was that if Kingsley's machine had led them to St Thomas church, with a secondary signal pointing to 30 Sanford Place, then he was the best candidate to engage in Henning's telepathy experiment. If he was already hearing voices in particular, then the chances of manipulating the signals by machine were greatly increased.

From an MI5 point of view, they were on track to wear down their man. To make sure he never left their sight, whilst letting him roam free in the world, they had mounted a massive ground operation. They'd had to move residents out of the way to make way for the legions of actors that were walking and driving the streets around him. As far as they were concerned, this was the most dangerous man on earth and they had to creep up on him slowly, rather than risking a confrontation by bringing him in. Their worst case analysis suggested that this was a person capable of *mind control*, and so the level of fear in MI5 was palpable.

Evenings and weekends were the most difficult to control. LJM had a habit of getting in his Land Rover Defender on impulse and driving off to goodness knows where. He frequently left an armada of vehicles in his wake because they simply couldn't predict where he was going to go. The best they could do was to stake out major junctions and roundabouts as an early warning system to get at least one vehicle in front. Roadworks sprung up everywhere, as a way of controlling traffic flow and catching LJM in their net.

Later that morning, Julia took another phone call from Jack. Once the call was done and having put the phone down, she was no longer in the mood for hiding information based on suspicion of a bugged office. So she announced a general meeting in the boardroom where she would brief the entire senior team about what was going on. This included Kingsley, Henning, Theo, and Nicky.

'I'm sure you'll have heard by now of the explosion yesterday while Nicky and I were tailing a man known as LJM. We've had confirmation that the bomb was set off deliberately by MI5. The same MI5 who gave me a badge. And the same MI5 who is listening to this meeting via bugs planted in this room,' she expounded.

There was stunned silence.

'LJM is a target identified by USA HQ. He has a long mental health history and is therefore believed to be highly sensitive to the kinds of signals sent out by machines. There is some debate as to whether we really believe the signals from Kingsley's and Henning's machines are similar. That said, there is sufficient momentum behind LJM's identification and his place of residence at number 30 Sanford Place, which corresponds precisely to the strongest signal in the St Thomas church results.'

'Jack wanted to begin the process of tailing him, and so I worked a twenty-four-hour surveillance shift the day before yesterday, prior to Nicky turning up. However, we were unaware that MI5 were one step ahead of us, and the explosion was sent as a signal to warn us off,' she continued.

'MI5 buy into the LJM identification and will take complete ownership of the ground operation to bring him in. We're out of the loop from here on. With the exception of the Kingsley and Henning experiments, which are ongoing. And software development will be continued by Theo. Nicky, you can either work for MI5 or go home. You can't stay here,' Julia finished her speech.

'If LJM works just across the stairwell, we just have to strike up a conversation with him and find out what he knows. What's the problem?' asked Theo.

'If you do that, you'll be shot. There's a sniper in this building. You've misunderstood the whole point of the data gathering process, Theo. It's imperative he doesn't know for sure that we're onto him until the endgame,' ruled Julia. Theo looked very sheepish.

'So basically most of us continue as we are. The person who's on dodgy ground is you, Julia. Is that correct?' reasoned Kingsley.

'Very perceptive. I think I need to take some time off. All of you will report directly to Jack in my absence,' concluded Julia.

Again there was stunned silence.

There was no getting away from the fact that life in the Exeter office wasn't the same without Julia. With only a couple of female developers, it became a very male-dominated environment.

Henning worked separately with the NHS to continue experiments in telepathy with his QE machine.

Kingsley worked with Jack and the British military to perform another experiment with his EM machine. They erected some hoarding on Sanford Place outside number 30. Then took up the paviours, dug six inches into the ground, cast a solid silver conductor plate, and assembled the machine on top. Lieutenant Orion operated the entire schedule based on the same settings as before, and Kingsley wasn't even required to turn up.

As expected, the results showed a split signal: a strong geographic signal towards the church and a weak biological signal towards the house. Kingsley realised this was the end of the road for his signal hunt out in the field. Only once LJM had been brought in would there be any hope of conducting an op inside his house.

Theo kept quiet about his brief to rewrite the software. The British line was that this was for the purpose of general improvements on existing hardware, whereas Theo realised its true purpose was to facilitate the miniaturised all-in-one hardware and software that didn't require a supercomputer. He wondered what was the point of relocating the entire software team to the UK, but reasoned that USA HQ must have been making some kind of goodwill gesture to appease the British.

When Julia returned to Exeter a few weeks later, she'd been stripped of her MI5 badge. Rather than walk into the office on a low note though, she thought she would go on one of her characteristic shopping trips. Rather than go to Blue Crystal which was a front for MI5, she went to the Crystal Shop on Gandy Street instead. She was in the market for some more crystal wands, and there were two examples in the window. One was called *tiger's eye* and was a swirling mass of whites and browns. The other one was called *jasper* and was a beautiful reddish orange colour.

She went inside and got chatting to the lady behind the counter. She was told all about the volcanic *larimar stone* from the Dominican Republic, about how it was found in only one place on earth. And then she heard about Exeter's volcanic past with cinder cones at Rougemont Castle and Brentor on the other side of Dartmoor, and how volcanism would return to the Exeter area once again in the future. So Julia bought a pair of earrings as well as the two wands.

When she walked into the Exeter office, it was to the sound of cheering and clapping. She blushed briefly and then settled down at her desk to begin the business of the day. She called a general meeting with Kingsley, Henning, and Theo, taking her goody bag in with her.

'Gentlemen, I won't bore you with stories about my holiday. Suffice it to say I've had enough time off and have brought you back some presents,' she said. They were all ears.

'Kingsley, you get the eye of the tiger. This represents Scientific Fact and Scepticism.'

'Theo, you get jasper. This represents Science Fiction and Belief. It also happens to be what the Red Indians used to make their arrow heads from, if you've read the *Song of Hiawatha*.'

'Henning, you get these lovely earrings for your wife. They're in a stone called Larimar. Could you do me a favour and swap these with the blue crystal wand on your desk, please?' she asked. Henning obliged.

'Henning, your wand represents Spirituality and Super-Human Communication.'

They all thought about this for a moment.

'I'm just going to pop out for a few minutes. When I come back, I'd like you all to tell me what you think is going on with the geographic signal in the middle of St Thomas church,' she emphasised.

SUPERVAN

Jack was offered the chance to inspect SuperVan before it was shipped off to the UK. It was a short-wheelbase white Ford Transit van, ready to be wrapped according to the "story of the day". It had been completely rebuilt from the ground up to a military specification. Based on a Titanium Space-Frame chassis that included a Faraday Cage for the driver and co-pilot, the entire thing could be operated without leaving the cab.

In the rear was combined hardware for both the Horlicks QE and the Khan EM machines. The floor had a bomb-bay-style opening hatch design which allowed the EM machine to be lowered on to the tarmac for ground contact. They had to dispense with solid cast conductor plates for the sake of mobile operation, so they used a tank of conducting GEL instead. This meant that SuperVan left a trail of slime whenever it was pressed into live operation, a bit like a high-tech snail!

Jack was seriously impressed. 'She's a beauty. I'd say she's good to go.'

*   *   *

The meeting in the Exeter office continued when Julia came back into the room.

'Julia, we've all had a think about this, and I'll summarise from a purely scientific point of view. The challenge we face is to diagnose whether the geographic signal in St Thomas church represents a Monopole or a Dipole. On the face of it, the results appear to show a trail which simply leads to a *dead end* in the middle of the nave. However, the directional signals from the EM machine as it currently stands are two-dimensional only. You get north, south, east, and west but not up or down. This leads to two trains of thought.

1. I design a new version of my machine to work with directional signals in three dimensions. This will keep me busy for some considerable time.

2. Meanwhile, we extend the analysis on the existing machine by running it backwards. Whereas we followed the trail forwards to Exeter, we should now follow it backwards leading to goodness knows where,' said Kingsley.

'From a *science fiction* point of view, there are many places we could take this. Maybe the signal represents a *monopole* in three dimensions but a *dipole* in extra dimensions. Maybe the trail leads to *parallel universes*. Maybe there's a *black hole* in the middle of the church, and we just haven't noticed. Or maybe there's a black hole at the centre of the earth,' postulated Theo.

'From a *spiritual* point of view, the trail has led us to a church. It depends on your faith as to what that really represents, so maybe we should invite VIPs from all faiths to tell us what they think. Looking at the tools you've brought to the table, I notice that they're all made of crystal. Again crystal represents different things to different people, so maybe we could open a debate about that. Likewise on the subject of ley lines, for me, crystals are a particular form of solid matter found in rocks. Kingsley's machine sends signals through solid rock, and one theory is that it does so by forming super-conducting lightning trails along the path. We should commission some detailed experiments to find out,' said Henning.

Julia was stunned into silence.

Kingsley spent the next six months designing a 3D signal variant of his EM machine. Actually that was a lie, it was a semi-3D variant because it would only analyse down and not up. This was down to the practicalities of a machine with a ground conductor. If Kingsley wanted to go up, he would have to operate in airburst mode like Henning had done with his machine. But he wasn't ready to do that just yet. In any case, he reasoned that if he tried a ground-based signal so far, it was more likely to be a dipole going down into the earth then suddenly going airborne. He was using the magnetic north/south poles as his analogy. As part of the design process, he had to take leave from the Exeter office and go on secondment back to the USA. Much of his time was spent interacting with the hardware team.

Theo wasn't best pleased because it meant much of the software had to be rewritten (again), to make the transition from 2D to 3D signal analysis. Likewise, the firmware for the control unit had to be revamped. Kingsley took on that challenge himself. For him, this was putting himself back on the front line in a way that he hadn't done since ground operations stole the show. He was really enjoying it. Apart from anything else, it made him feel more like a scientist and less of the "mad". Julia's assessment had struck home, even though he wasn't prepared to admit it at the time.

Henning, meanwhile, was pushing ahead with his new-found role as a consultant with the NHS. After much political in-fighting, they allocated the old Sports Hall in Wonford House as the new home for his QE machine. The operational procedure was simple. They called a fire alarm drill to clear the building of administrative staff and then ran the experiment while they were standing outside. They turned the power down accordingly and put the participants in the same room right next to the machine.

Henning had been given the files for Barney and George who were the two strongest receivers according to the original Cedars results. He then requested a single A-list celebrity as a candidate for strongest sender. He chose Stephen Fry on the basis that he also had bipolar disorder, and was delighted when he accepted the invite.

Henning was altogether happier conducting experiments in a controlled environment. Although he'd enjoyed his time as an officer in the field, he decided that ground operations weren't for him, and it was time to focus on his core strengths as a scientist. Given that his machine stirred up other people's minds, he was lucky not to have caught the *mad* label himself.

Henning was poring over his results when Kingsley reappeared in the Exeter office.

'Kingsley, it's lovely to see you back in the UK again,' exclaimed Julia.

'Thanks, Julia. It's lovely to see you too. How are you doing mate?' he turned towards Henning.

'It's been quiet without you. As it happens, I have some interesting results,' replied Henning.

'Go on,' answered Kingsley.

'We did an experiment with Barney, George, and Stephen Fry in Wonford House. Stephen wore a hood so Barney and George didn't know who he was. Both Barney and George mentioned him in conversation afterwards. Meanwhile Stephen has disappeared into his cave. He's currently in

France, hiding from the media as far as we can tell,' reported Henning.

'You just exploded Stephen Fry? He's a national treasure!' intervened Julia.

'I have to say it was unintentional,' Henning replied.

'Seriously, Henning, mate. You're going to have to go easy on mental health celebrities if this is what it does to them,' reasoned Kingsley.

'I'm one step ahead of you there. We're going for A-listers with a clear history. I thought I would start with the "top woman", so we've sent an invite to Madonna,' responded Henning.

'Are you nuts? The world will go mad if you explode her,' pointed out Julia.

'Relax. She'll be fine. Don't forget, I've done this thousands of times myself during development,' asserted Henning, confidently.

'What will she get for her participation?' asked Julia.

'It's a free trial. We've agreed to share a transcript of the results in return for voluntary cooperation. We'll add a clause to the section on possible risks in the light of the Stephen Fry result. But I'm sure he will be fine too, given time,' said Henning.

'So Stephen knows that Barney and George picked up his name by telepathy?' queried Kingsley.

'Precisely,' emphasised Henning.

Julia and Kingsley could start to see where he was coming from.

*   *   *

In USA HQ, Jack called a general meeting.

'Team, the news of the day is that we're restarting ground operations in Mainland USA. This time we're focusing on just the Khan EM machine, but it does mean that all the Hum reports and other control issues are going to be right on our doorstep.

'The future of the Horlicks QE machine rests on British hands. They're doing some controlled experiments on mental health patients and A-list celebrities, and we have sight of the results courtesy of Henning. So everyone is happy with that.

'The reason for picking up the EM trail once more is that Kingsley is bargaining on a dipole rather than a monopole signal in St Thomas church. He expects the field lines to go down into the ground, a bit like magnetic north, which means we're now looking for EM south by running the signal in reverse. This man is an absolute genius. And it means we're heading for the West Coast boys and girls, so time to take out your bermuda shorts and wax down your surfboards,' he concluded.

This was the first time Jack had delivered a speech in one hit, and he received a standing ovation.

On an altogether different note, SuperVan had been smuggled into the UK on a freighter. MI5 had grown tired of chasing LJM on a no-contact basis and had broken just about every moral rule in the book in their frustration. They'd literally driven him mad by bombarding him with mixed messages and living ground operations—none of which had been so far revealing in the hunt for telepathy. LJM even had a spell in the Cedars, suffering from psychosis as a result.

The prime minister, David Cameron, was adamant that LJM was just a member of the British public and not a terrorist as the Americans feared. He ruled that they weren't allowed to bring him in for questioning because he knew that the scale of experimentation the poor man would be subjected to would mean he'd never see the light of day again. So LJM was a free man who must never know his involvement at the end of the EM trail in Exeter. Of course the Americans didn't want to take no for an answer, so they sent in SuperVan instead, driven by Jeroen Mulder with Delia Sciuto as co-pilot. Its first port of call was with Ansell and Perosa in Torquay. They'd done a deal with a small local firm to work overnight during a fresh wrap every day. By sending out SuperVan in different corporate colours, they hoped that would be enough to throw MI5 off the scent. They also organised a warehouse on Marsh Barton full of white Ford Transits so they could press the panic button at any time, pull the wrap off, and hide for a bit.

Julia had met LJM a couple of times in the stairwell or while catching some fresh air outside. She knew he went running at lunchtimes three times a week but also knew that it would be more than her life was worth if she pushed her involvement. The MI5 bombing incident was enough to convince her of that.

Nicky had gone to work with MI5 in the hunt for LJM's mind. Julia had the occasional social call from, her but business was strictly off the agenda. Julia considered requesting leave from the Exeter office so she could join the team in the USA on the hunt for EM south. That would most likely put her back out in the field again, but at the cost of losing her role at EM north because she knew they would replace her. And it would compromise her relationships with Kingsley and Henning as inventors of the machines. Not to mention Theo too. Although she wasn't entirely sure why they were still in Exeter, she decided to stay.

*   *   *

SuperVan arrived on Sanford Place with the intention of covertly tracking down LJM. The Americans were watching by satellite but as far as they knew, the British were unaware of what was about to happen.

They parked in the far corner of Sanford Place, facing towards number 30 so they could see LJM come and go. The plan was to catch him on the way home from work, when they had advance warning of him arriving. Then they would unleash a combined EM and QE pulse which would both disorient him and electrocute him at the same time. That would answer once and for all whether the EM signal was originating from him as a person or his house. They watched him leave in the morning and then waited.

*   *   *

'David, it's Barack. We appreciate that the string of experiments with the Khan EM machine has come to an end with the trail leading to 30 Sanford Place. Can I enquire what you've done with it?'

'We've dismantled it and put it into storage,' replied David.

'Cool. We have a suggestion for an additional experiment as a background check. Would it be possible for you to set it up on Dartmoor, at the same location as the trial for the Horlicks machine?' asked Barack.

'Are you sure you're feeling OK? You're asking rather than pushing, and you want us to conduct an experiment in a safe, controlled environment?' asked David.

'It happens,' said Barack, innocently.

'Is there something I need to know?' asked David.

'We'd like you to do it on full power,' said Barack.

*   *   *

When LJM returned home from work, he walked straight into the SuperVan trap. They caught him in the middle of the road, where they could get a decent fix away from the house. Delia pressed Go. The EM machine sprang into action, sending ground lightning through the conducting GEL onto the brick paviours. At the same time, the QE machine sent an airburst signal that made Delia and Jeroen see stars, never mind LJM. For his part, LJM staggered, clearly under the influence of the lightning. Hopefully, the QE effects would make him think he was having a nasty turn. The effects only lasted for five seconds. As they were carrying the latest most efficient version of the hardware, the overall process was faster than the older ground-based models.

Once LJM had recovered and gone inside, SuperVan decided to leave quietly. The data was sent via satellite uplink to Theo's department in the Exeter office for analysis. They were not followed.

For his part, LJM was clearly unsettled that evening and decided to go out. He got into his dark green Mazda MX5 and drove off.

MI5 had maximised the security level on LJM, so he was followed everywhere by an undercover circus. He was observed on the way out, and the police helicopter was scrambled to keep tabs. The Americans were watching the whole thing by satellite but decided not to send in a tail because they didn't want MI5 remotely suspicious. SuperVan was their main ploy.

LJM crossed the River Exe and headed for Topsham Road. Then he headed for Exmouth via the same route that Julia, Henning, and Kingsley had taken, via Topsham. He parked up at Orcombe Point and was walking on the sand, just as they had done. The observers were not astute enough to realise that he was almost walking in their footsteps.

Once he'd chilled out, he walked up the ramp to the end of the road where the monument with multiple lightning conductors was located. He weaved in and out in an odd kind of dance.

The police helicopter didn't bat an eyelid because they knew his history and were used to his strange behaviour.

When LJM finished, he climbed back into his car and drove back as far as Countess Wear roundabout. The police were expecting him to head home and were surprised when he went into the Beefeater for a drink. When he came out, he refuelled at the Shell garage and then got onto Bridge Road. This was a perfectly plausible alternative route back to St Thomas via Marsh Barton, but the Americans sensed via satellite that something was up. They had a motorbike waiting at Dawlish roundabout. LJM then confused the police but confirmed American suspicions when he turned left towards Dawlish.

He drove all the way to Dawlish and turned around in the road by the red cliff railway tunnel. On the way back, he turned right towards Dawlish Warren. By this point it was dark and the police helicopter gave up the chase. They called in reinforcements, but the Americans were one step ahead.

When he parked his car, LJM didn't notice the motorbike pulling up at the same time. And he certainly didn't notice the gun case the rider was carrying on his back.

He took the wooden walkway towards the beach, left along the terrace as far as the sand dunes and then down to the water's edge. He walked past all of the groynes to the open sand at the far end of the spit. There was just enough light that he didn't need to use his torch. When he got to the point opposite Exmouth, he undressed to his underpants and hopped into the narrow channel between the river and the sea. It was cold.

The Americans were mildly perturbed by his behaviour, as reported by the biker who had seen everything. He was given orders to shoot and was assembling his rifle when the unexpected happened. A seismic tremor, the like of which had never been recorded in the Exeter area before, lasted for a brief second.

The gunman was given the order to stand down while they re-evaluated what was going on.

The *Express and Echo* was full of it the next day. All of a sudden, the previous stories and scaremongering surrounding The Hum were suspended. There was even an article speculating whether The Hum had a geological rather than a man-made origin. Julia was reading the newspaper when Henning and Kingsley arrived, having gone for a spin in Henning's Jaguar.

'Gentlemen, I'm glad you're here. There's been a new development,' she said.

They all assembled including Theo in the boardroom.

'Last night, we were observing LJM via satellite. He had a slightly bizarre trip where he went to both Exmouth and Dawlish Warren. At the point where he went for a swim in the river, a magnitude 4 seismic event was recorded, which is all over the papers today. Even on the way back, LJM took another bizarre route in Crediton and finally re-crossed the river at Bickleigh Bridge. He was also seen staring at the river from Thorverton Bridge before returning home,' she said.

Theo was aware of the SuperVan connection and had the experimental results in his pile of papers. But he also knew that MI5 had the room bugged. Although Julia was his manager and a known CIA agent, he was also aware of her previous MI5 connection. So he kept quiet. His USA contact for the top-secret work was always Jack. He resolved to ask Jack about Julia's current status.

'It seems that you're asking us whether LJM's activities could in any way be connected to the seismic event,' commented Henning.

'My take is that there are two possibilities.

1. The seismic events were already in progress, and LJM was following them on his travels.

2. LJM is super-human, and the seismic events are somehow following him around. He was at the end of the EM trail after all. Perhaps there is something mysterious at work here, and we're only just starting to scratch the surface,' said Kingsley.

Julia looked horrified.

'So are you saying that it's possible we are all somehow compliant in making this happen?' she summarised.

'Yes,' he replied.

'You're not normally that way-out-there with your analysis, Kingsley. Do you have any other evidence to back up this claim?' she observed.

'Think about what happened to Atlantis. Or the island that disappeared into the sea surrounded by a ring of volcanoes. It's entirely possible that civilisation is the *architect of its own demise*,' he concluded.

There was a stunned silence. And they sensed that MI5 was probably gob-smacked with that one too. Theo was looking distinctly uneasy.

Finally, Julia broke the tension. 'Well, it's funny you should say that because Mrs Springs in the Crystal Shop was telling me that Exeter is surrounded by eight volcanoes. She's expecting they will bring a new form of crystal to the surface, a bit like the Dominican Republic.'

CONSPIRACY THEORIES

After that, all hell broke loose on the conspiracy theory front.

'Barack, it's David. I'm sure you've heard that we experienced a seismic tremor in the Exeter area last night. This is starting to make your proposal for a high-power experiment on Dartmoor look distinctly suspicious. What are you trying to do to us?' he demanded.

'David, we had no idea this was going to happen,' answered Barack, truthfully.

'So how much power does "high power" really mean?' he asked.

'The whole thing runs off a standard 240V single phase power supply. Draw your own conclusions,' he responded.

Theo had the call with Jack where he asked about Julia. Jack answered him that Julia could be trusted but to get her off-site for a meeting where it wasn't bugged. Seeing as he didn't have a car, Theo thought he would ask Henning and arrange a meeting between all of them.

*   *   *

Julia meanwhile was invited to a meeting with senior management at the Met office.

'We're very pleased you could attend at short notice, Miss Barnes.'

'My pleasure.'

'We're aware that you're employed by the CIA, managing a team of highly skilled people in an office on Kings Wharf. We're also aware that you were a double agent with MI5 in the past.'

'That's correct. It was an open arrangement with full visibility on both sides.'

'Very good. The reason we've asked you here is that a damaging rumour has come to our attention via another inter-agency connection. The speculation is that the Met office were somehow complicit in causing the Boscastle disaster.'

'That's not something I'm aware of.'

'Do you have any comment to make?'

'Do I believe the Met office were directly responsible for Boscastle? Answer: no.

Do I believe that a localised weather event like Boscastle could be caused by cloud seeding or some other man-made technology, armed with sufficient information and timeliness? Answer: yes.'

As was typical with any meeting involving Julia, her remarks were greeted by silence.

'Thank you, Miss Barnes. That will be all.'

*   *   *

When Julia returned to the office, Theo intercepted her.

'Henning is offering to take us all out for lunch in his car. On your expense account, of course,' he grinned. Predictably they went to the American Bar and Grill at the top of Haldon Hill. Theo was hoping that MI5 didn't have it bugged.

Once they'd settled in and ordered food, Theo spilled the beans.

'The reason I've asked for this meeting is because I have some confidential information. While you lot have been swanning about, I've been working on a new version of the software that is suitable for miniaturised hardware. Well, the Americans have managed to squeeze all of the hardware into the back of a Ford Transit. They call it SuperVan. Anyway, they have one of them prowling the streets of Exeter. Yesterday they did a combined EM and QE op on LJM in the street outside his house. That was right before he took off and started to behave really weird,' he said.

'Very interesting. That adds a new dimension to the puzzle. So now the question is whether SuperVan caused the seismic event and were LJM's activities coincidental,' offered Kingsley.

'That's what I was thinking. Until I remembered that the results of the experiment show that LJM personally was at the end of the EM trail. It's a biological signal. Whereas the church was a geographical signal,' added Theo.

'Good lord,' said Henning.

It was Julia's turn to be silent.

When Julia contacted Jack, he brought her up to speed on the Met office conspiracy.

'One thing we've realised is that the Trans-Atlantic Cable surfaces in Widemouth Bay, which is seventy kilometres west of Exeter. This may be of some significance as to why the strongest receiver signal is located there. We don't currently have the technology to send a test EM pulse from USA with enough strength to reach Exeter. However, we can send one that will reach the town of Bude a few kilometres to the north. So with presidential permission, that's a test we could do that will give us some more information and not flame the situation in Exeter anymore. Also, it might help to draw the press off the scent. The only thing to be aware of is that there is a satellite communication station north of Bude, so we run the risk of taking out one of their satellites as collateral damage. Not to mention the spike on the carrier signal, which will be seen loud and clear by the Brits,' he explained.

'Also here in the USA, the decision has been made to use the latest hardware in the search for EM south. Which basically meant building a second SuperVan. It was shipped by military transport to Nevada and driven to Area 51, so they could re-do the original experiment as a baseline,' he continued.

'The power of the portable machine is less than its ground-based counterpart. And with a shorter battery-based pulse time, it could generate signals up to a maximum distance of twenty-five miles. However, armed with the experience of previous ops, they were prepared to drive 100 miles or more in the direction of a strong signal before trying again. Very rapidly SuperVan ended up in Los Angeles. They parked up at the sea front and engaged the EM machine by opening the hatch, lowering it onto the tarmac and filling the ground gap with GEL. There was no need for the QE machine in this instance. They pressed Go and sent the data to Theo for analysis. That's the latest status,' he finished.

Meanwhile, LJM was motivated to go on another of his little escapades. This time, he remembered the location where he'd encountered a large seal whilst out running with his running partner Martin. It was out on the reed beds on the way to Topsham. The RSPCA had been there, and their assessment was that this was an old blind seal that had come up-river on the tide and was just hanging around to have a look before the tide came back again.

Either way, encountering a wild seal was way out of bounds as a normal running experience, and it stuck in his mind. For some reason, today he decided to pick up the thread and revisit the place so he could pay his respects.

He drove to Topsham, parked in the car park, walked to the Lighter, and then walked upstream from there. It was about a mile and was a peaceful walk on a sunny day.

When he found the spot, he simply lay on the ground as if he was praying to the gods.

He gazed straight up at the sky and said, 'Hello, sky.'

No response.

Then he turned over with arms and legs spread wide, staring straight into the earth.

'Hello, world.'

He was absolutely gobsmacked when he got a reply back.

'Hello, man.'

He thought a bit, and the best he could come up with was that it seemed to be a female voice.

'Hello, Mother Earth'.

'Oh no, I am not Mother Earth. I am a *mother* and I walk on the *earth*. I am a woman.'

'Hello, woman then. Do you have a name?'

'Patsy'.

'Pleased to meet you Patsy. I am Bob.'

THE HUNT FOR EM SOUTH

Jack visited Malcolm's office. 'There's something that I need to tell you, based on where we've got to with the Met office. I might remind you that this is above the security level of any of your staff, so it goes no farther than you.

'Understood,' said Jack.

'There is a connection between the Trans-Atlantic cable and weather events in that area. However, it doesn't happen by using the EM machine, it happens with the QE machine. That's why we're very cagey about using it on full power.'

'Sorry, I'm not totally with you there,' said Jack.

'Do you remember Boscastle?' asked Malcolm.

'OMG, you caused Boscastle?' exploded Jack.

'You see why we want to keep it quiet,' explained Malcolm.

Theo pored over the results. 'That was predictable. EM south is somewhere across the Pacific. Next stop Hawaii then,' he muttered to himself, forgetting that MI5 were probably listening.

Julia decided she needed a private meeting with Kingsley, so she took him down to the Coffee Cellar, further along the quayside.

'Kingsley, there are a couple of things I need to discuss with you. Firstly, the British are considering doing an experiment with your machine on Dartmoor,' she said.

Kingsley's eyes widened.

'Secondly, there is a potential opportunity coming up in Australia, your home country. We don't know for sure yet, but the USA team is currently heading for Hawaii in search for EM south. Nobody expects the trail to end there, though. They're all looking at a map of the world 180° removed from Exeter. Apparently that puts you in the Pacific Ocean just south of New Zealand. If the signal from Hawaii comes back as expected they're expecting to pick up the trail in Sydney,' she continued.

'So you want me to conduct some more experiments then?' he said.

'Please bear in mind that the hardware has changed. The Americans have built SuperVan, and that's what they're using for the track to EM south. It's a much more efficient process and just depends on Theo for results analysis. I'm proposing that I should drive and you should operate. Or we could swap round depending on the mood,' she said.

Kingsley didn't take long to make up his mind.

'That's a serious offer. I'd be delighted,' he said.

'In the meantime, I'll see if I can get you on board for the Dartmoor stunt. They'll need you to redo the power settings anyway,' she finished.

When Julia got back to the office, an MI5 agent, Barbara, was waiting for her.

'I already handed in my badge. What do you lot want?' she posited.

'Can we talk in private?' she responded.

'Sure, the meeting room is free,' she offered.

Once they were seated and the door closed, the interview started.

'Please tell us about SuperVan,' she commanded.

'What can I tell you? It's a bit of kit in operation in USA. I've never seen it myself,' she answered.

'Where are they going with it?'

'That's private business for the USA.'

'So it won't be coming here then?'

'You'll be the first to know if it does.'

Barbara knew that Julia was holding something back but couldn't prove it. The SuperVan in USA was clearly nothing to do with UK, but the obvious come-on was whether USA intended to restart covert operations. Barbara was genuinely unaware that SuperVan had clearly landed in UK. Although MI5 had placed listening devices in the American Diner, the CIA had then wiped the place clean, in anticipation that Julia and her team would use it for a private meeting at some point. So the CIA maintained the upper hand at this point. Barbara went away with little more information than she arrived with. However, the threatening behaviour towards Julia was noted. The last thing the CIA wanted was for her to end up in a British jail.

Jack pondered his options and decided that pulling Julia out of UK was the best thing to do, at least while they were conducting covert operations. She was booked on a flight to Sydney and told to take a holiday before Kingsley arrived with SuperVan.

Julia took the opportunity to ask a few more questions and decided that she didn't fancy a trip across the Australian Outback in short-wheelbase Ford Transit full of techy kit. So she requested a redesign based around a motorhome.

In a spooky twist of fate, LJM decided to go to Martin's Caravans with his wife on Saturday morning. His out-of-the-box behaviour was noted by both MI5 and CIA. At that point, neither agency knew where he was planning to go. MI5 increased surveillance on LJM once more. CIA noticed and decided to hold back on any more SuperVan operations until the situation was resolved.

* * *

'David, it's Barack. We noticed that LJM went shopping for motorhomes. If he's planning on a trip, it's imperative we know where he's going, given the security surrounding this whole affair.'

'I agree, Barack. You'll know as soon as I know.'

'The consensus here is that if he attempts to leave the UK, we should bring him in for questioning.'

'That won't be happening, Barack. He's a free man and has done nothing wrong. The most sensible solution is to leave him alone.'

'In that case, we'll just have to pick him up when he lands in France or wherever.'

David knew he was snookered at that point. He could only guarantee LJM's freedom while he was on British soil. He wasn't about to invade France with a massive counter-security operation to keep the CIA at bay, so LJM would have to fend for himself.

The British were notified that Julia had already left the UK following the aggressive behaviour from MI5. And they were warned that Kingsley would be leaving soon too shortly, so please could they get on with it and organise the Dartmoor experiment.

At this point, it looked like the international cooperation was starting to fall apart and the future of the Exeter office hung in the balance.

*   *   *

Two days later, Kingsley was contacted by the Royal Artillery. They had assembled his EM machine on the firing range just south of Yes Tor, and he was invited to do the power settings training for Lieutenant Orion. He asked whether a separate Faraday Cage would be provided for him and was told he would be safe inside a heavy metal military transport vehicle. Kingsley got changed into his Army uniform and waited for them to pick him up.

Theo was complaining about having to do the analysis using the old software, and Kingsley assured him he would send a message to USA to deliver the latest hardware formally to UK. MI5, who were listening to every word, took that as a clear sign that they should push for delivery of SuperVan.

When Kingsley arrived on Dartmoor for the operation he'd envisaged, he noted the different nature compared to the Henning handover. A minimal number of troops were involved as they were clearly expecting to be electrocuted otherwise. Kingsley realised that on full power, his life depended on Lieutenant Orion. If she pressed Go before he was back in the transport, he would have a minute or so to live and understand that a kill order had been executed. He shrugged off the fear on the basis that he was probably still too valuable, even though he was clearly in British hands and the CIA were nowhere in sight.

'Good morning, Tania,' he decided to dispense with formalities.

'Good morning, Kingsley,' she responded.

'I'll crank you up to full power today,' he asserted.

'Loving it.' She grinned.

After the handover which took about five minutes, Kingsley walked the hundred yards back to the transport vehicle. He felt like he was walking the plank, but he made it OK. To his surprise they then headed out of the area. It was clear that the military weren't taking any risks, and Tania would be the only person left on North Dartmoor by the time they got back to Okehampton Camp.

The driver picked up the radio and announced his arrival. He was told to keep everyone inside. Kingsley hoped that he hadn't given Tania a death sentence.

She pressed Go and they heard a boom.

'OMG. I hope she's OK,' said Kingsley out loud.

The driver checked in.

'She's fine.'

'What was the noise then?'

'We just triggered a magnitude 5 seismic event in Exeter.'

For the first time in his life, Kingsley went pale. He knew that his relationship with the Royal Artillery had just been sealed forever. They were loving it, even if he wasn't.

When he arrived back in the Exeter office, Kingsley noted that both Henning and Theo were looking distinctly uneasy.

'What just happened?' asked Henning.

'A man-made seismic event,' replied Kingsley.

They all knew the implication.

Kingsley decided he would waste no time, picked up his passport, put on his motorbiking gear and went for a ride directly to Heathrow Airport. Both MI5 and CIA were watching him every inch of the way.

'How about a walk, mate?' Henning suggested to Theo.

Theo knew that the results analysis was completely redundant under the circumstances, so he just walked out with Henning.

Intuitively, they wandered in the direction of St Thomas, crossing on the north side of Exe Bridges and along Cowick Street.

When they got to St Thomas church, a police cordon with blue-and-white tape had been put in place. MI5 were too scared to send in the military in case it triggered another event. Henning asked what had happened.

'The church has sunk five feet into a sinkhole' was the response.

The policeman paused to take a call.

'I'm being instructed to ask both of you to leave the St Thomas area,' he said.

They did an about turn and walked back to the Waterfront restaurant for a pizza, while they mulled over their options.

*   *   *

'Barack, it's David. I'm sure you know what just happened. If you have a covert SuperVan on British soil, I'm ordering you to remove it now.'

'Understood,' conceded Barack.

The order was sent for SuperVan to get on the first ferry from Plymouth to Roscoff.

*   *   *

Jack considered his options once more. With Henning working separately with the NHS, Kingsley and Julia out of the country, SuperVan sent to France, and no realistic prospect of any EM experiments in Exeter now that ground lightning had been linked to seismic events, there seemed little point in keeping Theo and his team there. Nevertheless, to send that kind of message to the British at this delicate stage might further destabilise international relations, so he elected to keep things as they were.

MI5 were the first to learn that LJM and his wife were planning a trip to Portugal. They didn't know the exact route they would take, but putting two and two together, they decided the chances of their ending up in Roscoff under the clutches of SuperVan were way too high. So they escalated.

'Barack, it's David. We've learned that LJM and his wife are heading to Portugal, most likely via Roscoff. Can I count on you not to intervene, or do I need to flood the place with MI5?'

'This man is a terrorist, David. Look at the trail of destruction in his wake.'

'Barack, you were the one who ordered the high-power Khan machine experiment on Dartmoor. The cause and effect clearly has nothing to do with LJM. He's an innocent man.'

'Innocent maybe but still a terrorist. We can't afford to have him wandering the globe. The consequences are simply too extreme.'

David realised that they weren't going to see eye to eye on this one.

When Mr and Mrs LJM arrived in Roscoff, they drove their motorhome off the ferry and into an international incident.

For starters, the port workers had gone on strike and barricaded the vehicles in, preventing them from driving into France. There were tyres burning all around. The most imposing sight was an American military transport vehicle amongst the cars.

Then the place was awash with American and British 'Customs' officials.

Finally, SuperVan was parked in the corner, waiting, lurking.

The decision was taken to question LJM in a combined panel of American and British agents.

'Good morning, please take a seat.'

They sat down.

'We understand that you're on a trip to Portugal, is that correct?'

'Yes.'

'Is this business or pleasure?'

'We're going on holiday to a hot country in a camper van. Is that difficult to understand?' emphasised LJM, irritably.

'And you plan to return to the UK afterwards?'

'Yes.'

'Please understand that you won't be able to leave the port until the workers have concluded their strike. There's nothing we can do about that.'

'Understood.' LJM sighed.

'We'd like to question you on your state of mental health. We understand you have a bipolar diagnosis with borderline personality disorder. Is that correct?'

'Yes.'

'Do you suffer from psychosis?'

'From time to time.'

'Do you hear voices and see visual hallucinations?'

'Not all the time.'

'When was the last time you experienced anything like that?'

'Back in March.'

The questions dried up. They were not given the option to leave, and Mrs LJM started to become nervous.

After a while, an armed American soldier walked into the room with a number of his colleagues gathering outside.

'You're under arrest under anti-terrorism laws. You're coming with us.'

LJM was strong-armed out of the room and across the ground towards the transport vehicle.

At that point, there was a clear break in the chain of command because SuperVan unleashed its load. All of the soldiers were electrocuted along with LJM. Mrs LJM was stood farther away but was also caught. Needless to say she was terrified.

When the soldiers recovered, they continued on their primary mission. Once they were all inside, they drove through the line of burning tyres and headed south.

'Barack, it's David. I'm ordering you to stop what you're doing now. You've just caused another seismic event in Exeter.'

'Precisely my point, David. This man is a terrorist, plain and simple.'

'Barack, the one with his finger on the trigger is you. You're the one who has caused every seismic event in Exeter as far as I can see. You need to wake up and have a reality check now. You just kidnapped an innocent man and terrified his wife into the bargain.'

Barack was silent.

'OK, they can have their holiday, but my boys are following right behind.'

'Agreed.'

LJM was deposited by the side of the road and ordered to give up his camper van keys. He was told to wait there. His head was spinning and had no idea what just happened. The transport vehicle returned to the port, picked up Mrs LJM and dropped off a soldier to drive the camper van. They returned through the line of burning tyres once more, in convoy this time. When they arrived back to LJM, Mrs LJM was delighted and confused to be reunited with him. She demanded an explanation.

'You saw what happened to St Thomas church?'

'Yes.'

'We think that your activities are somehow related.'

'Seriously?'

'Yes. Please go carefully from here on. We will follow behind you.'

'Is this really necessary?'

'There was another seismic event in Exeter twenty minutes ago.'

'Oh, I see.'

Mrs LJM wasn't pleased with the idea of a holiday with American military in tow, but decided not to argue given that they'd only just got their freedom back.

* * *

'Barack, it's David. I'm hearing reports that you used SuperVan on LJM and that caused the seismic event in Exeter. Please tell me this is wrong.'

'It's correct, David. The experiment was done on French soil. We had to find out whether there was a connection via him personally. There clearly is. He's now officially the most valuable man on the planet. Everywhere he goes, he has military protection. Is that understood?'

'That's a new definition of freedom.' David sighed.

* * *

Mr and Mrs LJM carried on the rest of their Portugal holiday without event. The military did their best to remain inconspicuous. At one point they were camped out on a strip of land next to the Guadiana River, owned by another British couple. Mrs LJM liked the idea of growing vegetables and living the quiet life.

Unknown to them SuperVan was also in tow. David Cameron was appalled when he found out, but there was nothing he could do. The Americans really did have him over a barrel for as long as LJM was not on British soil.

When they returned to Roscoff, SuperVan parked in the car park while the camper van and military transport got on the ferry.

David realised their intention was to implement military protection on British soil and given the SuperVan connection, he wasn't going to argue. The last thing he wanted was another international incident surrounding LJM. So he let that one go and told the British military to stand down when it came to protecting LJM.

'Barack, it's David. Under these circumstances, I think you should pay for the damages to St Thomas church. We're going to demolish it, reinforce the foundations and rebuild it stone by stone in a sympathetic fashion.'

'Agreed.'

*   *   *

When Kingsley arrived back in the USA, he was greeted as a hero.

'Establishing the causal link between ground lightning was a master stroke. You're a genius,' said Jack.

'I have to say I didn't know that would be the result. We're lucky in a way that it came through so clearly,' said Kingsley.

'And without damaging any US property.' Jack grinned.

'Is there any chance I can inspect SuperVan before we head off to Australia?' asked Kingsley.

'There's been a slight complication. SuperVan got rejected and is being turned into SuperCamper as we speak. Call it female input. Julia didn't fancy travelling the Australian Outback in a short-wheelbase Ford Transit,' replied Jack.

'How will that work?' asked Kingsley.

'We were scratching our heads on that one. The best we could come up with was to use a model with a garage area at the back under the main bed. We've had to make some compromises. You'll have a EM machine but no QE machine. On the other hand you'll have a bigger GEL tank for more experiments.'

'GEL?' asked Kingsley.

'We're using conducting GEL in place of a solid cast ground conductor,' said Jack.

'Of course,' replied Kingsley.

Kingsley boarded the next flight to Los Angeles and from there to Sydney.

When he arrived at Customs, he was taken aside and quizzed about his visit.

'I'm an Australian citizen, you muppets,' he hissed.

'We know that, sir. Are you here on business or pleasure?'

'Pleasure. I'm going home for two weeks and then heading out for a camper-van trip with my partner, if you must know,' he replied.

'Thank you, sir.'

Kingsley thought it was all a bit odd and surmised that MI5 must have got involved. SuperCamper was a better camouflage than SuperVan so hopefully that would throw them off the scent. In any case, it would be arriving by freighter in two weeks' time so he could relax until then. The Americans were even arranging for him to 'buy' it at a regular shop. And it was a right-hand-drive version too.

Towards the end of his two weeks off, Kingsley met Julia at a café on Sydney harbour.

'Hi, genius,' she said, giving him a peck on the cheek.

'Hi, sexy' he replied, noting her new suntan.

'So do you fancy a camper-van trip with me?' She smiled.

'I have to hand it to you, that was a smart move,' he said.

'There are more than enough berths so you can have a bed to yourself if you like,' she said, touching on a subject they hadn't discussed.

'Is this business or pleasure to you?' he asked.

'Both,' she replied.

'I see,' he observed.

'I fancy the pants off you in case you were wondering. But if you want to keep it strictly business then that's fine,' she added.

Kingsley thought about it for a while.

'How about I ask you out to dinner and you can tell me all about you. Personal stuff. No business. We could call it a first date,' he offered.

'I'd be delighted. And you can pick up the bill for a change.' She smiled.

Kingsley and Julia started SuperCamper operations in a car park in Sydney. Everyone was on edge waiting for the results, because if, as predicted, the signal originated in the ocean south of New Zealand then further operations in Australia would be limited.

As it happened, the result came back that the main signal was to the east, which meant that the EM south signal was to the west, in central Australia. Kingsley and Julia set about preparing SuperCamper for an extended trip across the Australian Outback.

Meanwhile, LJM and his wife had finished their Portugal holiday and had returned to the UK. Both Americans and British were absolutely paranoid that something else was going to happen in Exeter as a result of their return. In the event, they drove into Sanford Place, parked their camper van, and were able to take a look at the demolition work going on in the churchyard, without further ado.

However, there was no getting away from the fact that having the American military accompany them on holiday, as well as escort them on the return home, was an unwelcome intrusion into their lives. As far as LJM was concerned, the governments were paranoid and had leaped to an insane conclusion by assigning any responsibility to him.

Mrs LJM was particularly dissatisfied and demanded that they go on another holiday to get over the one they just had. In an attempt to pick a location as far away as possible from the events in Exeter, she came up with Australia as the destination. One of her family members had relocated to Alice Springs, so the obvious choice was to visit there first and then carry on to Sydney after that.

Jack was almost beside himself. 'We've just arranged to send SuperCamper heading west from Sydney and at the same time, LJM and his wife decide to arrange a holiday to Alice Springs? What is going on? Has the whole world turned up the level of synchronicity so we get these amazing coincidences?'

'No idea, boss,' conceded Albert.

'Barack, it's David. I hear that LJM and his wife are heading for Australia for another holiday. Surely you're not planning the same level of military intervention as the last one?'

'No, we've decided to back off on this one. I've taken on board your comments about us being the ones with our finger on the trigger, and we're going to take a more laissez-faire approach with EM south. With the portability brought by SuperVan and then SuperCamper, it's logistically a lot easier for us to cross Australia than it was to operate in the UK. We'll have agents on board, but in essence we're proposing that Mr and Mrs LJM turn up at the same time as Kingsley and Julia, then we'll see what happens.'

Once Kingsley and Julia had got into the swing of things, they could conduct an experiment, take a reading, get the results analysed and then move another 100 miles east to perform the operation all over again.

LJM had managed to get time off work, and since Mrs LJM ran her own business, she was able to take the time off whenever she wanted. Their holiday to Australia was booked, and they got on the plane destination Alice Springs. They had no concept of what was going on the ground and the extent to which it related to their experiences in Exeter.

In the event, Kingsley and Julia traced the EM south signal to Alice Springs at the exact same time Mr and Mrs LJM turned up at the airport.

The signal was more diffused than the one in Exeter, so they didn't get a definitive fix on a building such as a church. The closest they could get was the Rock Bar on Todd Street.

Sure enough, Mr and Mrs LJM naturally made their way to the bar without any intervention from the Americans or British. The level of spookiness was so off the scale that it effectively humbled everyone into submission. Kingsley and Julia were already waiting inside when the LJMs walked in and approached the bar.

The barmaid was free and went over to serve them.

'Hello, I'm Patsy, can I help you?'

'Pleased to meet you, Patsy. I'm Bob and this is my wife Sue.'

Mark Ridler was diagnosed with unipolar disorder (depression) in 1998, following the death of his first child. He spent three months in Wonford House in Exeter, receiving cognitive behavioural therapy and a series of antidepressants.

He fought to come off the drugs and was basically fit and well for the next fifteen years.

Then after divorcing and remarrying, he experienced a sequence of very stressful family-related episodes. These led to increasingly manic behaviour with psychotic symptoms too, throughout 2013.

In 2014, he was admitted to the Cedars, diagnosed with bipolar disorder, and prescribed mood stabilisers and anti-psychotics.

The mania continued, resulting in a Section 2 detention, a criminal conviction, and divorce for the second time.

In 2015, Mark was admitted to a mental hospital once more with continual delusions and hallucinations, believing that Madonna wanted to marry him. He was only able to make progress when he realised that the voices in his head were fiction. Once he'd made the decision not to hear them, then normality returned.

Mark has subsequently achieved good health, albeit with an ongoing underlying depression. He was admitted to the Cedars with a dose of mania in late 2016 and to the Littlemore

Mental Health Centre with another dose of mania in early 2019.

This book tells a fictional story of the CIA and MI5 battling to stay one step ahead in the face of two new technological inventions based on psychological effects. The trail has led to the historic town of Exeter, where the CIA are experimenting on the general population and the Cedars mental hospital in particular, without British consent.

After the initial frenzy, MI5 get the measure of what is going on and a complex international situation develops, where David Cameron and Barack O'bama cooperate for a while, before competitive tensions emerge once more.

The CIA opens an office in Exeter where the main characters Julia Barnes, Kingsley Khan, Henning Horlicks, and Theofanes Raptor lead the charge. Their antics regularly bring them moral dilemmas as a result of their work. And it forces them to think long and hard about what their technology is really telling them. Conspiracy theories abound.

The hunt focuses on the 'Leather Jacket Man' or LJM, who has a bipolar mental health profile and lives close to the epicentre and the end of the trail, St Thomas church. His character is based on the real-life experiences of the author, including psychosis and paranoia that develop as a result of him believing that security services were following him around.

In the final chapters, a new mobile technology called SuperVan hits the streets and is used to follow the trail in reverse, starting in the USA and ending up in Australia.

LJM discovers the answer to the question of telepathy, but keeps it a secret from the CIA and MI5. Until next time!

Printed in the United States
By Bookmasters